Soul Sex

A Sexual Adventure Through the Chakras with Erotic Escapades in Exotic Lands

Pavitra

Published by ShellDen Publishing

This is a work of fiction. Names, characters, places and incidents either are products of the author's imagination or are used fictitiously. Any resemblance to actual events or locales or persons, living or dead, is entirely coincidental.

Warning: This book is sexually explicit and may cause an increase in body temperature, blood pressure and heart palpitations. Read at your own risk. Please note, it is always advisable to practice safe sex and use protection.

American Address:	15600 NE 8th St. B1, # 654
	Bellevue, WA 98008, USA
Canadian Address:	101-1001 W. Broadway #341
	Vancouver, BC V6H 4E4, Canada
ORDERS:	1 866 SoulSex (1 866 768 5739)
WEBSITE:	www.soul-sex.com

Book Design by Scribe Graphics Inc., Victoria, BC, Canada

ISBN 0-9684928-2-7

DEDICATION

To my beloved, my twin flame, the other half of my soul, my lover, my companion, my playmate, and my trusted friend. Thank you for following your heart that lead you to me and a togetherness and joy we have searched lifetimes for.

To all those still searching for that perfect one – never give up your desire to be fulfilled on all levels. It is possible, it is real. First you must discover who you really are, express that as fully as you can, honor and love that being that looks back in the mirror, then and only then will you be able to share with another on the same frequency.

To the power of music and movement, and rhythms of the land and cultures that have shaped my own learning, I thank you.

To my connection with all that is, to all that helps create this wonderful existence called life, to which we are all connected, all one – I give thanks.

Pavitra

TABLE OF CONTENTS

FOREWORD

Sex. Most of us do it. Many of us enjoy it, or wish we did. Yet there are so many stigmas and judgments surrounding this perfectly natural act. Most of the time it takes place behind closed doors with all sorts of pleasures, frustrations, questions, inhibitions, yearnings, fantasies and so much more, left unspoken. This is not so for Pavitra. Nothing is taboo as she takes us on an erotic adventure in her search for fulfillment on all levels, or Soul Sex. That is, satisfaction gained through activating all our energy centers, or chakras.

Do not expect a deep, intellectual approach to the chakras or sex. Soul Sex is fiction and is written in a very light, easy-to-read style. Pavitra draws upon the images and associations of the different chakras in every scene and explicitly describes her sexual encounters. At the end of the adventure are practical exercises - if the steamy fiction has not already given you plenty of scope to explore your hidden desires. And do not miss Pavitra's rudiments of wisdom along the way for living a truly happy and fulfilling life.

Soul Sex bridges the gap between spiritual enlightenment and the carnal pleasures of the flesh. It is written by a woman who obviously stands in her truth. Self-assured and confident, Pavitra has an incredible energy and passion for life, which many wish they could also have. In Soul Sex she writes with an open heart, speaks her truth and shares the very core of her being. If you read her simple tale with an open heart and mind, you will perceive the depth beneath the simplicity and realize she offers the key to what can make you shine and achieve fulfillment on all levels.

Karen Farley,
Editor-in-Chief, Lifestyle magazines
New Zealand

INTRODUCTION

"Soul Sex" is an erotic fantasy fueled by my overabundant imagination. By reading these fantasies and sexual escapades it is my intention that your own fire be lit, your imagination runs wild and you get inspired to bring some of these ideas into your own relationships to activate and awaken your chakras and sexual desires.

It has been said that many girls in China who were to be born in the year 1966 were superstitiously aborted. The communities knew the power of the year of the Fire Horse and dared not risk the potential chaos a woman born of that year would bear upon the community.

Full of fire, a horse at full gallop, with no rider at the helm, I jumped into the world in that year. Experimenting with anything and everything right from the word "go," is it any wonder that I would travel the world, seeking the answers to life's many questions, searching for a love so powerful, so rich, so meaningful that my soul would feel satisfied at the deepest level possible? Searching for a rider who could enjoy the ride, allow me my freedom and cherish the flight through the dark night of the soul on into the light.

Having looked through many windows and walked through many doorways, I finally found my way back to myself. The key for me was to move the energy, to free my body, be all I could be. Through movement and music, sexual playfulness and travel I found my connection to all of what I am and with that, a connection to another aspect of my soul through whom I have found the ultimate sex of all, "Soul Sex."

Let these pages take you on a journey; a passionate, sexual journey through the chakras (our energy centers), into exotic continents, sexual escapades, into fantasies you can recreate in your own lives to enhance your experience called "life" and bring back some of the wonder and joy of being alive, of being you – a beautiful, sexy, sensual, powerful, passionate, heart-centered, expressive, aware, tuned-in YOU. You are all of this and more. Experience it!

I really started to tie everything together when I was exploring the seven energy centers (chakras) and subtle energy bodies through dance in India. I realized that as I focused on the first chakra, my sexual desires were more raw, physical and earthy. As I moved up into the second chakra my desires changed and I searched out sensuous, sensitive loving. When I reached the third chakra I needed hot, powerful, full-on sex, yet when I was working on my fourth chakra that type of sexual encounter basically revolted me! I needed the heart connection, the security of feeling at ease and under no pressure to perform. When I reached the fifth chakra I felt the need to connect with someone with whom I could communicate verbally my desires and make lots of noises while making love. The sixth chakra was different again, I longed for that third eye connection, the feeling of being bathed in purple light as I orgasmed, the urge to be the light. When I was focusing on my seventh chakra I wanted a very meditative lover, one with whom I could lie there in union, listening to the silence, becoming one breath and feeling my connection to all that is.

Such totally different loving on each level! It was amazing how my needs changed as I focused on my different energy centers (chakras). We are all of these types of lovers. Sometimes we are more centered in one chakra than another. It is important to experience and activate each and every chakra in order to fully experience life and loving. Once we have truly activated each center then we can choose which one or which ones we want to transmit and receive on, for in essence that is what a chakra is – a transmission and receiving center.

It is fascinating to look at our relationships in this light. With some friends we to go on trips into nature (a first chakra activity), others we contact when we want to go out and feel romantic, enjoying the sensory delights of food (a second chakra activity). Sometimes we want to get motivated to simply have a good time and feel our sassiness (a third chakra activity), and at other times we want to just hang out and read a book or cuddle up and watch a movie (a fourth chakra activity). There are times we really just feel like having a good old chat with someone (a fifth chakra activity), and there are certain people we like to do more spiritual or enlightened activities with, such as yoga or meditation (a sixth chakra activity) and still others with whom we feel really comfortable just being with in silent contemplation (a seventh chakra activity). That is why we need many different friends, companions and/or lovers.

Unfortunately, in our society, these different needs are not recognized and partners get jealous if we go out and spend some time with others (especially those of the opposite sex). Yet it is totally understandable when you realize that we all have different needs and that it is very rare to find one person who can meet all of those needs. However, it is possible to find that one person, as I have, and if you do, you are very blessed.

I feel that we require activation in our lives on all levels, on all chakras. If we deny or suppress one aspect we are denying the possibility of achieving our true potential in this lifetime. That is the reason why so many people do not stay in their relationships. They are often judged harshly for moving on (especially if children are involved) but in these times we, in essence, have the possibility of experiencing many different lifetimes in one life rather than taking ions to move through our issues. This may mean changing partners and experiencing what we have to experience with them and then moving on, thanking them for what they have allowed us to share and learn.

When we think of our relationships in this way it is easier to see why we were attracted to a person in the first place, whether we are still compatible, and what needs to be worked on with regard to activation of particular chakras and areas of personal growth. With greater understanding about the chakras, we may be able to grow more in the relationship, rather than move away from it. As we understand our own needs and desires and where we are at (chakra-wise) we can focus on our own needs, empower our own chakras, encourage our partners to do the same, and then reassess the whole situation.

Maybe, simply by activating each chakra with the fun, playful, sensual suggestions outlined in this book, your relationship to yourself and your loved one will blossom also. Then again, maybe you will realize on which levels (chakras) your relationship is not connecting and allow each other to explore other ways of satisfying those chakra needs.

In my own life I experienced many different connections with people on each and every level until I found one with whom I resonated on all levels. When I met my now life-partner, the bells and whistles went off, the earth moved, a lightening bolt struck me and I knew deep within that this was the one.

The love I share now with my beloved continues to grow and get better every day. When we make love, I feel like a virgin each time, experiencing the wonderment of sensation, of every cell coming alive, of a connection so deep that our souls can fly limitlessly high. We love, laugh, play, talk, write, ski, travel, debate, grow, share, and experience the heights of orgasmic ecstasy every day. I give thanks, every conscious moment, for the beauty and completeness of our love - a love on all levels. I have called this book "Soul Sex," which is what I have discovered with my beloved. In essence, "Soul Sex" is that which connects the spiritual with the physical plus all the pieces in between.

I have formatted this book in line with the seven chakras (energy centers), combining the seven colors (red, orange, yellow, green, blue, indigo/violet and white), with the elements (earth, water, fire, air, sound, light and ether/ consciousness) and the sensations (physical, sensual, powerful, heart-full, verbal, insightful and peaceful), with stories set in different countries (Australia, Africa, France, Jamaica, Germany, Ireland, Egypt, England, Nepal, India, and New Zealand) interlaced with experiences relating to each chakra (walkabouts, mud, waterfalls, food, dance, massage, steam, heat, horse-rides, mountains, meditation, chants and breathing) and music that resonates with each energy center (dijaredoo, drumming, romantic, reggae, classical, techno, love songs, ballads, chants, Indian, New Age) and of course, SEX on *all* levels.

Reading this book is a fun way to learn more about the energy centers, about conscious sex through the chakras, about passionate adventures to exotic lands, about rhythms and cultures, music, rituals and dance. It is possible to have experiences that relate to each of the chakras in any country and with any individual regardless of their cultural background. I do not intend to offend anyone or place people or countries into any boxes or stereotypes. These are simply fantasies modified to fit my chakra outline.

I hope you get excited by what you read and stimulated on every level so that you can get the most out of this wonderful experience called "life." Love is magical and when we find that connection on all levels within ourselves, then we can share that with others and enjoy "Soul Sex" - the ultimate experience.

CHAPTER ONE

❤ *First Chakra Activation in Australia* ❤

Color: Red
Element: Earth
Quality: Raw & Physical
Music: Dijaredoo
Activities: Nature, Mud, Walkabout
Physical Location: Legs, Base of Spine

Having just completed my University studies I desperately felt a need to reconnect with the earth. My head had been stuck in books for five years and I had become waterlogged because of the drizzle and rain which typifies the weather in my hometown.

The only thing that kept me going during those long hours of study were the foreign films I escaped to go and see at the Film Society each week, or the three day film festivals I would immerse myself in three times a year.

I lived at what seemed like the bottom of the earth… you couldn't go much further or you'd hit Antarctica. I lived vicariously through the movies I watched and fantasized about living in those cultures, experiencing the land, meeting those tall, dark, sexy men with the melting tongues and accents.

I dreamed of traveling to far off lands and exploring ALL that those places had to offer. I wanted to feel the energy of the land in each place, taste the fruits and delicacies of each culture, dance to the rhythms and music of the people, and feel what it felt like to make love with different people from different cultures. I wanted to wake up from my dreams and experience the reality of this beautiful planet.

When I graduated from university, I immediately packed my bags and took off on my adventure around the world. I wanted to experience it all, live life to the fullest and decided never to say "No" to any opportunity that came my way; to make the most of life's gifts and explore everything.

First stop was Australia. I yearned for the warmth of the red soil. I wanted to feel myself connected into the Australian land and take my head out of the clouds it had been stuck in for so long. Tired of sitting in my chair with my head in my books, listening to the rain on the roof, I wanted to stretch my legs, free myself of the load I was carrying on my shoulders and get back to nature.

I decided to go walkabout which is a traditional thing to do in Australia. You simply take off into the unknown with no map, no plans, and just see where your feet take you. I had never done this before, but it felt like the perfect thing to do to start the energy flowing through my body again; to fire my body up and free my mind of all the intellectual stuff that had filled it in the last few years. I needed to physicalize my energy into my body, into the earth and come back to the true me.

Walking barefoot across the Australian outback, I started to feel my connection to Mother Earth being rekindled. The red soil caressed my feet, gently making it's way slowly and seductively into and through the small crevices between my toes. So soft, so warm was her touch, I became absorbed, lost in the feeling of being… an ancient connection to Mother Nature welled up from the depths of my loins.

As my eyes drifted up from my bare feet I became aware of the material that clothed my body, separating me from nature's gifts. With urgency, I tore at my clothing, throwing it to the wind, reveling in the warmth of the sun's rays bathing my skin. The air between my legs gently caressed and cooled my pussy. Lifting my arms to dance above my head, I invited the breeze to seductively touch every inch of my bare skin as it absorbed the droplets of sweat from under my arms. I drifted into oneness with the sky, the sun, the wind and the earth herself!

Reaching down I penetrated and immersed my fingers in the soil. Ah, the ecstasy as the red earth ran softly over my hands. Sliding and going in deeper, I felt the warmth of her touch spread up my arms. Joy rippled through my body as my bare breasts came under the spell of her warm radiance. Stretching my arms out in front of me still further, my nipples made soft, brushing contact with her red warmth and instantly became hard and erect. Mmmm, so warm, so inviting.

Sidling up to her like a snake, my belly touched hers, my pussy reconnecting with her womb, my thighs tingling as contact was made. I felt like a virgin yet the feeling was familiar. My face gently touching hers, I smelt her earthy aroma and, allowing my tongue to slowly extend from my lips, I tasted her essence.

Rolling over I wiggled my bottom into her earthy heat. Feeling the orgasmic sensations start at the base of my spine, I bared my buttocks down even more and felt the warmth of the red soil as it made its way between my cheeks. Arching my back forward, I felt a powerful shaft of energy shoot through me as the open, wet lips of my pussy made contact with her fire. I was in heaven yet this was very much earth.

Enjoying her embrace, I rolled and rolled, grabbing handfuls of her, I rubbed her warmth all over me, into every pore, every crevice, over my breasts, my pussy, between my legs. I was in rapture as I became one with her.

The intensity built and I began to moan and the heat began to rise in me. Rubbing and rolling more and more vigorously I felt the sensation of orgasm grow from deep within. My moaning became more and more intense and I screamed out loud as the energy increased. I kept it building by fingering my pussy and pulsating my buttocks back and forth. Squeezing each breast in turn with one red earth-covered hand, while the other desperately sought the secret depths of my vagina, I brought my energy to such intensity that I felt completely out of control. I had lost myself to the earth; I was one with her. I felt her fire as she yielded to my movements and she welcomed me deeper and deeper into her soul. "Yes, Take Me!" I screamed as the energy rolled up through my body and I surrendered to the rawness of the convulsing waves of my orgasm…

The warmth of the sun had started to wane as I slowly drifted back into consciousness. Lying naked and tingling with an euphoric afterglow, I felt my continued connection with the mother energy that had embraced me.

In my semi dream-state I began to become aware of a distant sound, an earth tone, a deep, low sound that pulsated through the soil. Rolling gently over onto my side, I pressed my ear to the ground and felt its vibration. It sounded so far away, yet felt so near.

Allowing myself to become the sound I traveled in my mind's eye through the earth, following the rhythm up from the soil, through the termite-eaten branch, to the lips of the man kissing it. I felt his breath as he breathed life into the wood making it resonate with an old, deep overlapping rhythm that reached in and touched my core. It felt like he was breathing life directly into me, and my body started to vibrate in response.

As if in a trance, my body slowly lifted up from the ground, growing like a seed into a plant that sways gently in the breeze. I felt mesmerized as I was drawn to its source. With eyes closed, my feet softly seeking the earth, one step at a time, the vibration guided me to its essence. The sound called me, drawing me into its aura. My soul, pulled by the breath of the man, connecting to me through the sound of dreamtime.

Magnetized by the deep, pulsating rhythm, my body developed a yearning, a yearning to feel the vibration within me, to feel the breath of life flow through me. As the sound and my yearning grew in intensity I dropped to my knees and crawled as far as I could until I could go no further.

I became still, immobilized by the sensation as the vibration came in waves through my body. My forehead touched the earth in reverence, my arms outstretched before me in gratitude. What a gift this day had been. What a wonderful trip back to the mother, back to the source.

There on the earth with my knees curled up into my chest and my arms outstretched, the vibration seemed to travel up and down my spine activating my kundalini. The energy surged through my body in waves reawakening the cells deep within my sex. Oh the bliss, it kept coming and coming, higher and higher! I felt my body quiver, my pussy on fire, then the energy exploded through my body like rolling waves of orgasmic juices. "Thank you! Thank you!" I cried, as the orgasm pulsed through every fiber of my being for what seemed like an eternity.

Finally, with the orgasm subsiding from within and as the rhythm of the music faded into silence, a blanket was gently laid over my limp and spent body. As I sank into a blissful sleep curled up on my side, I was aware of a strong male energy moving close to me and folding his arms around my grateful body.

I felt safe and secure in the arms of my mother's brother. Like a baby curled up in a cradle. "No fear, fear no fear, love is everywhere, love is here…" my inner voice sang to me.

Awaking to the sound of crackling twigs, I gently opened my eyes to see the stunning outline of a male figure gazing into the fire. His body shone, glistening in the glow, every muscle outlined perfectly in the moonlight. His skin - black as black could be. His features intensely beautiful as he looked penetratingly into the fire.

Feeling my energy as I looked at him he slowly turned his gaze to meet mine. So deep, so still, so calm, so strong – those eyes. I conveyed my gratitude to him for looking after me with a slight nod of my head. He held my gaze steadily, not saying or intimating anything – just a strong, steady gaze. I admired his serenity, his contentment with who he was. I allowed myself to go deeper into his eyes and felt his connection to his source. It ran very deep. His connection was deep, deep into the red earth.

As I watched him watching me I could feel a movement within my soul. It started from the very depths of my being and ignited the woman within me. As I maintained eye contact with him, I could feel a reciprocal movement from deep within his soul.

My juices started to flow as my fire responded to his stirring passion. His strong, lean body rippled with power and I could sense the strength of maleness that my femaleness longed for. My breathing increased, forcing my naked breasts to rise and fall as his gaze penetrated me. I longed for him to go deeper and deeper into my being. "Yes," my eyes conveyed, "Yes!"

Together, as if by silent command, we both effortlessly rose to our feet. I, standing naked but for the blanket draped over my shoulders. He, with only a loincloth around his middle, modestly covering his very manly private parts.

Not losing eye contact for a moment, we moved slowly towards each other, our bodies longing to connect, my hot, wet vagina willing me towards his penis. The yearning to have a strong, male member penetrate my now dripping, red-hot pussy was almost overwhelming.

As his hands touched my body, I felt my sex almost squeal for joy. How I longed for this big strong man to take me there and then, in Mother Nature's backyard, under the moonlight, beneath the stars. Yes! He felt my desire and I could sense his excitement building.

We stood there face-to-face, chest-to-chest, my breasts just touching his. I could feel his penis, erect under his cloth, pressing against the bush above my ripe and open pussy. He reached behind his back and moving his pelvis back slightly the cloth around him fell away effortlessly to the ground. My heart missed a beat as I caught a glimpse of his incredible member. I gave a slight shrug of my shoulders and my blanket fell revealing my tanned, wanting body.

It was as if some powerful force was pushing us closer and closer. I edged my pelvis closer and felt his penis, erect, powerful and strong push against me. I could not resist any longer, I was on full burn. I had to have him in me. The urge was overwhelming as my hands reached around his waist, grabbing him and pulling him against me.

The pressure of his hardened penis against my mound was almost too much. I went weak at the knees and his arms gently guided me onto the earth. My legs parted effortlessly as his body came down onto me and his wonderful penis slid into my very welcoming pussy.

Strong, powerful and hard, he plunged into me. Like nothing else I had ever experienced, the rawness of that moment was awesome. I felt his muscles rippling and taunt, as he drove deeper and deeper, penetrating my innermost realms. It felt so good to have such a real man enter me, shaft me so physically, so completely!

My legs opened wider and lifted higher as his thrusting grew in intensity. I could feel my body respond as groans of ecstasy left my mouth. It seemed to turn him on even more and he thrust even harder and faster. "Yes!" I cried. It felt so good to be thrusted so forcefully, so vigorously!

I thrust back and arched my back higher so as to receive his full quota. He enjoyed me responding and thrust even harder! Boy! I had never experienced such raw loving!

I was about to let my orgasm blow when all of a sudden, he withdrew leaving me hanging at the edge. I was about to scream for more when he thrust his penis into my open mouth and spurted forth the creamiest, sweetest, tastiest substance I had ever had. A wonderful protein milkshake! I gulped it down, licking his gorgeous penis of every last drop, squeezing and sucking at it as my body rose to new heights. I exploded into total orgasm with both hands clasped around his penis and my mouth burying into every last inch of his hardened shaft. My body lurched and convulsed as I drove my head up and forward, seeking more of his shaft in my mouth with each wave of orgasmic energy that continued to roll through my body.

As my orgasm subsided, I lay back feeling the energy pulse and tingle throughout my body. Looking up I saw the first colors of the sun's morning rays light up the sky behind the glistening body of my black-skinned lover. Gazing deeply into his eyes, I conveyed my gratitude. He nodded in response as I allowed my mind to drift back over the wonderful night! I felt so blessed, and look, I said to myself, the dawning of another beautiful day! I wonder what gifts it will bring? I closed my eyes again so as to fully savor the afterglow sensations of the total activation of my first chakra.

The gentle rocking that my new friend was doing to me brought me back to the present. He beckoned me to follow him. Gathering the thin blanket, I wrapped it around my middle like a sarong. My feet reconnected with the soil and I could feel the night's coolness slowly make way to the warmth of the new day. We walked in silence as the sun rose in the sky.

An hour or two must have passed as the earth and the day were getting warmer and the thirst I was starting to feel made me think of water. My friend stopped and motioned to me to look beneath a stone he had lifted. There below was a small pool of water that I thirstily drank from with my hand. It was as if he had read my thoughts and manifested my desires instantaneously.

Furthering our journey through the magnificent outback I started to notice a change. There seemed to be more vegetation and I could feel some humidity in the air. We rounded a large rock face and there before us was this spring fed mud pool. Reddish brown, slimy, wet mud!

Entering the mud pool, my friend motioned to me to join him. Well, I thought, this will be a new experience! Swimming in mud! Releasing my blanket sarong, I lowered my naked body into the cool mud. Wow! What a sensation, I thought. I watched in wonder as my friend gathered up handfuls of soft mud and spread it slowly and deliberately over his body.

This I have to experience, I thought to myself as I ventured forth into the depth of the pool. Simply walking into the mud pool was outrageous! It squished between my toes and I could feel the slipperiness as the mud spread up over my legs. I bent over and felt the texture of the mud with my hands and rubbed it over my arms. Reaching down deeply into the cool, slippery semi-liquid, I pulled it up and spread it around my upper legs and pussy. It felt so amazing! I quickly gathered up more handfuls and spread it over my belly and rubbed it around my breasts! Ooh! What a feeling! So smooth, cool and slippery!

Absorbed in my own mud bath I never noticed my aboriginal friend as he came over, until I felt the mud on my back. His strong hands moved softly over my bare skin as he spread the mud all over my back and down around my bottom. How wonderful! With more handfuls, he spread the mud up over my shoulders, down under my armpits, and around to my breasts, as I turned to face him to allow his hands full access to the front of my naked body.

I, in turn, reached down, scooped up the soft mud, rubbed it onto his torso and then, reaching behind him, spread it down over his tight buttocks. I felt his bottom twitch in pleasure as I smoothed the mud around and around his cheeks, making sure to slide my finger down the crack. I continued down the backs of his legs and then made my way up the front. With great handfuls of soft, damp mud I made my way slowly to the top of his legs, pausing to feel the strength of his upper leg muscles as he opened his legs to a wide and inviting stance. Filling my hands with more mud I spread it on up to his beautiful penis. Wow! It had felt good last night and now I knew why, I thought to myself! What an incredible specimen!

As I honored his penis with my hands, appreciating the mushroom shaped head, I marveled at how responsive it was to my touch. It grew as I caressed and honored it. With one hand holding his hardened penis, I rubbed his fine chest with the other in amazement at the perfection of his human form. He seemed to enjoy me appreciating his body and his penis responded even more so by getting bigger and bigger!

He removed my hand from his penis. Stepping back from me, he took his big, stiff woody in his own hands, and lovingly rubbed it as if it were his best friend. He proceeded to continue honoring his whole body while

I watched. It seemed to be a self-love ritual and boy did it turn me on. I loved to watch him loving himself and I started to touch myself in response. I wanted to feel the magnificence of my body, with its feminine curves and silkiness. I rubbed my hands slowly over every part of my naked, but mud-covered body, around my buttocks and up over my breasts, consistently spreading the soft, moist, cool mud.

Wow! I never knew it could feel so good to lovingly touch yourself, being consciously aware of every little curve and groove. What a turn on! Loving and touching myself was turning me on as much as he was turning himself on by loving his body. Far out! I was getting juicier and juicier and he obviously was getting more and more horny too.

We kept playing with ourselves and touching our bodies while watching each other until it got to be too much. At this stage he was lying on the bank masturbating himself. His hard, erect penis was sticking up in the air – I just could not resist! I jumped on him – his penis just sliding right into my juicy, wet pussy. Wow! I rode that boy for all he was worth until we both slipped back into the mud.

I rolled over on my belly and pretended to crawl up the bank teasing him with my wiggling behind, which of course he could not resist. In anticipation I awaited his shaft of energy to penetrate me from behind. I was not disappointed! With full force he re-entered me and pushed me more up the bank with each powerful stroke, I loved it!

We played for what seemed like hours, taking turns to touch and shaft each other and ended up lying on the bank in blissful exhaustion, feeling the sun bake the mud hard onto our skin. Such a strange sensation when it dried! It became so stiff and hard. Quite bizarre I thought as I stood up – weird how it all sort of cracked! Then I smiled as I looked down at myself. Youch! It even hurt to smile.

I looked over at my friend who laughed. He got up and motioned me to follow him, I did, very slowly – it felt so strange, like I had armor on. We walked a short way and then rounded another rock face into a small canyon where just below us was a clean, clear, blue pool of water. We carefully made our way down the bank and thankfully immersed ourselves into the water.

What an incredible feeling. The clay turned back into mud, the mud dissolved into the water and my skin became silkier than silk. It felt as though I had been reborn. My skin was softer than a baby's and my hair amazingly light and fluffy. Who needs modern toxic, chemical-based soaps! These Australian aborigines sure knew a thing or two, I thought to myself. How come we lost it all? I asked myself as I let the lukewarm water carry me away to another world, to another time.

After my nature bath, my aboriginal friend pointed

me in the direction of a nearby town. I could see the buildings in the distance and obviously he did not want to venture into that concrete jungle where the people lived so far removed from his world. I thanked him by giving him a big hug and wandered off towards the town. I hitched a ride back to where I had left my belongings in storage and ventured off onto the next stage of my world travels.

CHAPTER TWO

❤ *First Chakra Activation in Africa* ❤

Color: Red
Element: Earth
Quality: Raw & Physical
Music: African Tribal
Activities: Walkabout, Dance
Physical Location: Legs, Base of Spine

I had always wanted to visit Africa as I loved the music and the African people I had met looked so powerful and strong within themselves. The men had the most spectacular physiques of any race and the women had such a strength about them that was almost scary to this little Kiwi girl. They knew what they were about and they took no bullshit from anyone!

I decided to fly to Senegal in West Africa and venture out on another walkabout with only the clothes on my back and the lightness of my heart. The freedom of taking of taking off into the unknown, unsure of my destination, following my inner urges, trusting divine guidance, gave me such a feeling of liberation.

A friend of a friend told me about a powerful man who lived in the jungle. Knowing only a handful of words in the local dialect, Wolof, I managed to ask simple directions towards the village. I received some strange looks – a white woman alone, heading out into the jungle, but they politely pointed me in the right direction. I walked through the jungle in the direction shown and found my way to a white sand beach that stretched for miles and miles into the distance.

What freedom! I stripped off my clothes, wrapping them into my sarong and tying them around my waist. Like a horse that had been fenced in for too long, I stretched my legs and galloped at full speed along the water's edge. The wonderful feeling of being naked empowered me as I ran and walked, walked and ran, feeling the layers of heaviness leave my shoulders, returning to my natural state.

It felt like I had been on that beach for an eternity. It was nearing midday and my tummy started to rumble in slight hunger. On the horizon I saw a small stream of smoke wafting into the air. As I got closer I thought I had better drape my sarong around my naked body. I curiously approached, then walked into the backyard of a small beach hut. There was a man smoking fresh fish. He looked up in surprise. I do not think he had ever seen a white woman in these parts, yet he greeted me warmly and invited me to join him for some food. I graciously accepted and relished the freshness of the sea's bounty.

In my broken "Wolof" I explained I was on a journey to visit a friend, and named the village. His eyebrows raised in disbelief saying it was a long way to go. I thanked him for the food and asked him to point me in the right direction. He beckoned me to follow him further up the beach to where we met a river and then told me to wait for a boat to take me to the other side.

Patiently I sat there enjoying the serenity of being on my own, out in nature, wondering what the rest of the day would bring. Hearing voices, there appeared out of the mangroves a dug out canoe with several people aboard. When they saw me their conversation stopped and they literally rubbed their eyes!

In my broken dialect I explained where I was headed and after much discussion and looking towards the sun, a lady stepped forward and indicated she would show me the way to the next village, then in the morning I would be able to complete my journey. After crossing the river we walked off into the depths of the jungle. My guide had just returned from the city, many, many hours away, where she had sold her palm kernel oil at the market. Both of us were feeling tired after our long day so we mostly walked in silence, appreciating the jungle sounds, the birds busily talking to one another as they nested in for the night, darkness settling around us.

Listening carefully, because at first I thought it was my imagination, I could just pick up the beat of distant drumming. The comforting sound of dwellings and people not too far away eased any thoughts of a long night's walk. As we got closer, the drumming intensified and soon we arrived into a village atmosphere of celebration.

As I walked around, taking in the sights, smells and sounds of the village festival, I noticed the women sitting in a circle, talking amongst themselves and looking my way. I was invited to join in the feasting and hungrily ate the sumptuous natural bounty.

After the feasting had finished, I noticed the women talking amongst themselves and giggling, as if in some secret discussion. They then motioned to a young man with a strong, firm body. He stood up proudly and walked confidently toward the women who then motioned me to come forward. I stood up and moved into the center of the circle, not knowing what to expect. However, it was not long before I found out. Apparently it was ritual in their village to honor any guest who arrived, with the company of a village member for the evening. Normally any visitors in these parts would be men, so it was the most succulent woman who would be chosen and offered to the male visitor. However, in my case I was to be gifted the most virile young man of the village for the night.

A little surprised but excited with this offer, I looked the young man up and down. He was certainly a fine specimen of manhood. They had chosen well. He was in his prime, about nineteen or twenty and so proud. Truly the African men loved and respected their physicality. Their bodies were so physically perfect, their muscles toned from their physical lifestyles, their dark skin smooth and silky. What an honor, I thought to myself!

The women were anxiously awaiting my decision. I nodded and smiled my approval and a sigh of relief went around the group. The villagers then gathered and formed a circle as the drumming began in earnest. The young man, my gift for the night, stood in the center of the circle and tuned into the rhythm of the drums. Slowly his pelvis started to rotate seductively in time with the drumbeat, making small circling motions as if to activate some hidden sexual power. It seemed to work, I felt my own body responding to his seductive motions and looked on in appreciation.

This show was for me. It was his way of showing me how good he was, how well he could move his body and his pelvic area. And I must say it moved very well! Unlike a lot of western men that's for sure! I felt my body respond, my feet finding it hard to remain still with the drumbeats intensifying.

Like a peacock, he strutted his stuff, building up the power and energy of his movement as the drumming increased its intensity. Prancing around the circle showing off his impeccable physique, the villagers clapped him on, expressing their approval with hoots and hollahs. Suddenly, he turned towards me, making eye contact. Wow! I had not expected the intensity or energy of his stare. It was a powerful invitation, a deep penetrating gaze that looked right into me.

My breathing quickened as he walked towards me, holding his hand out in invitation. My heart missed a beat! Now it was my turn to join him in the dance, I thought, to see if we were really matched. As my hand went out to his, he effortlessly pulled me to my feet while holding his intense eye contact. As my feet connected to the earth again I felt the rhythm enter me, activating a primal sexual urge to express my sexuality in this sacred time-honored way – through dance.

Slowly, I started circling the energy in my hips with small contained movements, showing the control I had of that area of my body. Wearing only my short, tight sarong, with my bare breasts highlighted by the flickering light thrown out from the cooking fires, I activated each muscle in my near-naked body starting from my buttocks. Turning and swaying, I danced in the center of the circle, to the accompaniment of the drums and my man's penetrating gaze. I knew it meant a lot to exhibit the power contained within the female body. I played with it and taunted him with my first chakra.

I felt the heat begin to activate my kundalini and the familiar surge of energy traveled up from the base of my spine. I started to undulate my back and he responded in like, moving closer and closer until his gyrating pelvis connected to mine and we became one with the movement. Undulating in time to the drumming I felt the energy surge between us. It was good, but not so fast I thought, and gently withdrew, deciding to raise his fire even more.

It became a game of showing off one's wares, showing what we both were made of. Did we fit? Did our bodies respond to the come-on of the other? This is how the people in these parts decided in advance if they were suited to each other energetically. Could I match him? Did he have enough durability to last the night? Were our rhythms compatible?

This was fun. It involved the whole village and encouraged the open expression of the inherent sexual nature of our beingness. It was exhilarating to feel the support of the villagers, their focused attention on our physical union. As we built our energy by dancing, the drumming intensified and the villagers moved in closer and closer, forcing us to become so close that our bodies connected as we continued to gyrate and pulse with the energy of the drums and our physical union.

Dancing with our bodies locked together, we became one beat. Suddenly a group of men surged forward and lifted us off the ground. Joined together, they lifted us high into the air and walked in time with the rhythm, circling the villagers, exhibiting our physical union. The villagers cheered and we were carried off away from the drumming towards a thatched hut that had a lamp burning and mosquito net draped from the roof over a mat on the floor.

Placed gently on the mat, the men of the village left, closing the door behind them. The rhythm continued as the rest of the village started to dance and pound the soil sending the powerful sexual energy deep into the red earth, enjoying the physicalness of being alive...

Dawn was breaking as I awoke, still wrapped in the arms of my virile young man, our naked bodies still closely entwined. What an amazing gift, what an amazing ritual, I had been blessed to be part of!

After thanking my bedmate, I set off into the new day bathed in red and orange morning hews. I walked for what seemed like an eternity and was beginning to wonder if I had missed my turning when all of a sudden I heard the laughter of women. As I rounded a bluff at the head of a valley I saw two happy, vibrant women working in a field. It looked like an abundant crop as it was standing well over a meter high. As I got closer I realized it was a big field of marijuana they were tending.

Smiling, they greeted me and expressed their delight when they heard the name of the person I wanted to visit – it was their brother. Now I know why he was so respected and well-known. He was the biggest marijuana grower in all of Senegal. The women saw my gaze wander to the massive heads on the crop. What a bumper, I thought. They motioned me over to their mat and lifted it, showing me the biggest bud I had ever seen.

"Would you like to try it?" they asked.

"Sure," I responded. They rolled me a small cigarette and I sat in the midday sun savoring the sweet taste.

Suddenly the sensation hit me and I felt it take my consciousness to another level. The colors intensified and the clouds took on many different symbolic shapes. It felt like the birds were conversing in perfect English and the plants in the field were dancing happily before me. I sat on the mat with the two village woman while the world exploded into multi-dimensional wonderment around me. Wow - this was good stuff! It was some time later that the women pointed me in the direction of their village and I headed off feeling a deeper connection to the nature that surrounded me.

Entering the village I saw two small children playing with ants. I stopped in wonder as I watched them totally immersed in the tiny ants' activities. No expensive toys to play with, only what nature provided, and even the smallest things offered time absorbing interest. I observed them quietly, amazed at how content they were with the simplicity of their existence. Then I continued, finding my way to the home of the man I had ventured out to meet.

A woman met me at the door and motioned that he was having his afternoon snooze.

"Would you like to have one too?" I was asked. Why not, I thought – that must be the tradition here. So I nodded my acceptance to her proposal. I was guided into the room next door which had a mosquito net draped over the bed. Choosing to sleep naked I let my sarong drop to the floor and relaxed my tired body onto the bed. I drifted off into an unusual half sleep, aware of chickens running through the room and the laughter of children playing outside.

Waking after an hour or two, I realized it was dark outside. I stretched, groggily got to my feet, and reached for my sarong. Wrapping it loosely around my waist, I wandered out towards the fire and drumming. Glancing around at the gathered villagers, my eyes stopped at the most impressive man I had ever seen. Long, jet black, matted hair streamed from under a Humphrey Bogart hat. With his dark suit jacket and a white T-shirt underneath, he cut a fine picture.

Overwhelmed by his obvious stature and standing in the village, I waited for him to invite me forward. He was clearly a man of presence and well-respected in his community. He nonchalantly looked my way and with a slight tilt of his head motioned for me to come to his side. The little child sitting on his right stood up and offered me her place.

I greeted him in my broken Wolof to which he

responded in perfect English asking who sent me. When I mentioned Lilou, his face softened and the most beautiful smile spread across his face.

"My brother," he smiled. I knew Lilou was not really his brother but they obviously had a very strong connection. With this now recognized connection, I was instantly welcomed into the village family. He called out to the people around and introduced me as Lilou's sister to which the people responded warmly. I liked this extended family idea. It felt good. We chatted as we sat mesmerized by the fire, then the familiar drumbeat started again. The children formed a circle and started clapping and dancing.

I watched for a while and found myself tapping my feet. One little girl noticed my response to the music and invited me to join them. Finding any music hard to resist I accepted and eagerly joined their circle, clapping my hands in time as each one jumped into the center and let the music dance them. It was a pleasure to be part of such a joyous bunch of kids. So many of the young people in the west are bitter and negative, dependent on TV and video games for their enjoyment. Not here. Here, there was a vibrancy and spontaneity that seemed to be missing in the west.

As my turn came nearer I could feel that familiar feeling of the drumming taking over my soul. I felt myself power up and let go into the moment as I stepped into the center. The energy in the middle of the circle was fiery and intense. It was easy to ignore the fascinated eyes of the villagers looking on. I slid into the rhythm and felt my feet connect with the heartbeat of the land. In reckless abandon I felt the music enter my soul. The drumming intensified as the drummers sensed my abandonment.

As the drumming got faster and faster, I felt my soul surrender into ecstasy, sweat dripping from of every pore, my bare breasts glistening in the moonlight. I let go into the moment, feeling the familiar energy rise from the base of my spine. The coiled kundalini snakes unwrapping and rearing their heads, as I became one with the rhythm. Dancing myself into ecstatic bliss I continued until I could dance no more and collapsed onto the ground.

A woman came up to me with a bowl of cool water and small cloth. Inviting me to drink the fresh water from the gourd, she then poured water onto the cloth and gently caressed my forehead, soothing my sweating body with its coolness. She carefully used the cloth saturated with water to cleanse my pores and awaken my body from its euphoric state. Then she guided me back to the side of the man I had traveled so far to meet. He welcomed me into his arms and held me close.

I could smell his beautiful body odor and felt the strength of his arms around my shoulders. I felt safe and secure. He spoke softly in my ear that he enjoyed watching me dance, that obviously I was an intense lover who surrendered totally to the moment. His voice had such a strong resonance, a vibration that entered and touched my soul. My body responded by melting closer into him. As the drumming slowed at the end of the next dance my host held up his hand that commanded instant silence. Then, in a loud voice so the rest of the villagers present could hear, he stated that I must be feeling a little tired and that he would take me into the house to rest. Willingly I surrendered to his will.

Effortlessly he picked me up, cradling me in his arms as he carried me towards the sleeping quarters. It felt good to be supported by this big, beautiful man and I felt honored that he would invite me into his home. Placing me down at the low door he guided me into the room I had rested in earlier that afternoon and confidently undid my sarong. He looked my body over admiringly and proceeded to remove his suit jacket and T-shirt. The muscles in his arms were impressive. As he removed his clothing my heartbeat increased. If his presence was anything to go by, what would his equipment be like? A little nervous I awaited as he dropped his trousers. I took in a breath. Yes, very impressive!

He sat me on the bed and proceeded to kiss my nipples, arousing an intense heat within my body. He made his way down to my pussy and took a deep appreciative breath in through his nostrils. Looks like my body smell appealed to him too, I sighed in relief. His tongue searched my clitoris and tickled it erect. This was an experienced tongue and I was enjoying the mastery this man exhibited.

Letting go I felt my body shudder in delight as my arousal intensified. He gently rolled me over and massaged my buttocks and pussy with his big, black hands, relaxing and opening my vaginal muscles even more. It felt good to have my body loved and honored. I let go into his hands and moved appreciatively, working my knees up under me. I wanted to help spread my vagina as wide as possible because I knew his penis would need lots of juicy, wet, slippery moisture to enable it to enter.

This man treated my body with the utmost reverence. I felt myself opening in anticipation as he climbed up onto the bed. I could feel that he was aroused and arched my back opening my vagina appealingly. Gently, yet firmly, he pushed his maleness into me. Slowly parting my vaginal walls little by little with each firm shaft, I felt my body relax, enjoying the sensation of such a perfect specimen of a man sharing his body with mine.

He pushed deeper and deeper, my body responding with oohs and ahhs. He adopted the rhythm of the drums outside and maintained his consistent, firm, powerful shafting for a long, long time. He was focusing on building my arousal more and more. The master of his own energy, it felt as if he was in service to the female species, that it was his duty to serve me and serve me well, to have me come stronger and more intense than I had ever come before. He was good!

I climaxed and climaxed, enjoying every wave of energy pulsating throughout my body. I could feel him getting closer and closer to ejaculating and my body yearned for him to explode in me; yet he withstrained himself, building me to a higher and higher plateau. His thrusting intensified as he used the full length of his massive penis in masterful thrusting strokes. He withdrew it right to the end and every time he thrust in, my pussy arched up towards him as the feeling of him entering me again and again made me yearn for more. Every cell in my body was on fire and I was wild with wanton desire. His pounding, the sheer shafting he was giving me, filled my pussy like never before.

I screamed in ecstasy and thrust my vagina hard at him with every stroke of his penis. Clamping my pussy around his penis as he withdrew to increase his desire, I built him as he built me. My body was about ready to explode! I sensed him close to firing his milky juices into me, so I opened my pussy more, taking him into me with a force that propelled his shot. In one blinding flash of light I felt the heat and energy of his milky semen shoot into my oh-so-wanting pussy, with the force of a million stallions. I collapsed exhausted onto the bed, quivering with the bliss of being soooo well done. I was one woman who was truly fulfilled and satisfied to the max! I lay there, unable to move, in total orgasmic bliss.

That was incredible, I thought as my mind came back

to me and started to function. I lay on my back, my legs still apart, weak and limp. My pussy was hot and juicy with love fluid slowly oozing from its still very open lips. I drifted off into the deepest sleep I could remember…

The cloudless morning dawned as I awoke to a myriad of village sounds. I slowly pushed myself up off the bed and my body instantly reminded me of the fabulous loving I had experienced during the night. My legs were weak and I steadied myself against the small bedside table as my body quivered in delight of the memory. My God, I thought to myself, that was some night.

Attaching my sarong around my waist, leaving my breasts bare, I ventured out into the sunlight, leaving the love hut in search of some water to wash myself. The village women quickly gathered around me full of wonderful big approving smiles and I was pointed in the direction of the washing place.

Returning to the village after washing I found the women had prepared hot tea that I was invited to share. The children kept coming up to me and touching my blonde hair, and then running away giggling. Obviously my blondness was quite out of the ordinary! Finishing my tea, I thanked them all and was accompanied by the women and children as I headed towards the boat for my return journey.

What a night, what a man, what an experience! The power of his physicality was perfectly manifested through his sexuality and my body remembered every sensation to its very core.

A deep sense of satisfaction and relaxation permeated every pore of my being. I knew there was more but was forever grateful to the beautiful man who had awakened my base chakra and connected me to the essence of the earth so totally. I thanked him silently with all my heart and waved goodbye to the villagers as the dug out canoe glided me away.

When I returned to Dakar (the capital of Senegal) after my walkabout, I realized that I needed to manifest some more money in order to continue my erotic explorations into the exotic realms. In true first chakra survival mode, I risked all by investing my last dollars in some wild African materials. Creativity is the life force of the second chakra. Letting it flow activates that particular energy center, so I shifted gears and moved into second chakra mode. Unleashing my creativity, I made colorful patchwork clothing to sell on the markets in the South of France.

CHAPTER THREE

♥ *Second Chakra Activation in France* ♥

Color: Orange
Element: Water
Quality: Soft & Sensual
Music: Romantic French
Activities: The Sea, Moonlight, Jacuzzi
Physical Location: Reproductive Organs, Belly

The Cote d'Azur always had a romantic ring to my ears. A romantic holiday destination for the rich and famous, I was sure to make my fortune there selling my wild African clothing, and I was looking forward to relishing in the splendors of the French Riviera. Upon arriving in Paris I immediately took off on my next adventure into the second chakra, heading south towards the white sand beaches and sexy Frenchmen, famous for their sensuous loving.

On arrival I discovered Le Marché des Artisans in

Nice where I could sell my creations each evening. By day it was the local fresh produce market selling everything imaginable. The market was a feast of vibrancy, life and color. The sweet aromas of the exotic fruits were enough to make anyone's juices start running. I licked my lips imagining the juicy contents and visualizing my body responding to the life force as the soft flesh slid down my throat. The sensuousness of fruit is incredible. I was getting turned on just being around all the different smells and visual delights.

I loved the banter and free flowing innuendoes from the people selling their wares. As I passed by one gorgeous-looking man, he grabbed a mango and pulled its flesh apart. It looked just like a woman's juicy vulva.

"Certain fruits are good for ze women," he said, "Zis one helps to make you very, very succulent," he said, with a twinkle in his eye. I replied that my juices were running very nicely, thank you very much, and inquired about his, as I picked a banana off his stall and seductively peeled its skin off. Then, sucking lusciously on it while holding eye contact, I rolled my tongue around its end and slowly moved it in and out of my mouth.

It was hot and I was steaming! Leaving the sexy stallholder full of desire, I ran laughing from the fruit stalls and made my way to the beachfront, a block behind the market. Stripping off down to my G-string, I dived into the Azur blue waters, hoping to cool off. I felt the water caress

my body and lingered there savoring the moment. Softly
from behind me, a familiar sounding sexy voice called out
"Mon Cherie." I recognized it as the man from the fruit
stand. He must have followed me to the beach, I thought.
I smiled to myself at his spontaneity. He had followed his
instinct and rushed after me, leaving his brother to tend
the stall. I liked his tenacity, and was turned on by it.

He swam up behind me and sliding his hands around
my rib cage he seductively reached for my bare breasts.

"What a beautiful, luscious pair of juicy fruits you
have there," he said in a sexy French voice. God, I loved
the French language. It was enough to turn anyone
on just listening! It was a hot summer's day, my body
was immersed in water, but I could feel the heat rising
within. I lifted my arms above my head to give his hands
unrestricted access to my naked breasts and body as I
wiggled my bottom back into his already hardened penis.
God I thought, here I was with a sexy Frenchman making
a come on to me in the sea. He had no qualms about doing
so in public, and I certainly was not going to stop him. I
was having fun!

Alluringly, as he pressed up behind me, he said in his
sexy, French accent, "I see you like bananas – would you
like to try mine? It is very long and straight. It goes very
well with a juicy, ripe, fleshy mango."

My juices started to flow as his voice caressed my
ears. I could feel his breath on my neck as his hands

explored my practically naked body. He gently slid my G-string aside and rubbed his 'banana' up behind me. As his hands moved up to my hips I leaned forward to make my pussy more accessible. Grasping me tightly, he lifted me slightly and guided my pussy onto his banana. As I felt his penetration I lifted my legs up and forward, dropping my bottom down in the process and effortlessly devouring his banana completely with my juicy pussy. God it felt good.

Making love in water was a new experience, and in public. The French were certainly a lot more open about these things! We were not exactly surrounded by people and we were far enough away from the beach so as not to be too obvious, but it was still the middle of the day, at a downtown beach. It thrilled me to be so explicitly open, to be in the Mediterranean sea, with a sexy Frenchman gently shafting me. What a great introduction to France!

I enjoyed sitting on his banana, feeling the sea supporting me and aiding the effortlessness of the moment. I became one with the water and imagined myself a dolphin in the sea, making love on the waves.

Pierre, I later discovered was his name, was always able to seduce me with his sexy French accent and subtle innuendoes. We had fun using fruit as the medium in our sexy communication and expression, especially in public. We spent many hot afternoons experiencing each other's fruits in and out of the water that summer. My relationship to fruit will never be the same! Everytime I see a banana I am reminded of his beautiful piece of fruit and mangoes make me juicy even thinking about them!

In the evenings the fruit and veggie market became The Artisans' Marché, where people of all nationalities sold artistic creations to the multitudes of tourists who were wandering the boulevards, enjoying the coolness of the night air. People loved my bright wild creations that I brought back from Africa and in the spur of the moment bought things they would probably never wear again after that holiday.

The European market was such that if something cost you a dollar to make you could charge ten, so the profit was good and in three months I could make enough money to travel the rest of the year. I loved the freedom to incorporate my theatrical skills in harnessing people's attention, my personal growth work in building their self-esteem, and my creativity in making things 'work' on them. It was like a theatre show every night and I was the lead actress, and the public was my interactive audience.

One evening I noticed an austere, well-dressed older man watching me. After some time he came up to me and remarked in a cultured French accent, "You could sell a fridge to an Eskimo!" Looking at him I gave him my biggest, succulent smile in thanks. Just holding eye contact long enough to be seductive, I turned to tend to other customers.

The reason why I was so successful selling on the market was because I had fun and enjoyed my work. It also gave me permission to flirt and everybody likes to think they are desirable. Something I learned in Africa was that there is no point doing something unless you did it with love. I loved what I was doing and so that energy permeated every interaction. People basically want to be noticed, communicated with as human beings, and to have some interaction on a personal level. My having fun and flirting, and not just the hard sell, showed people that I was genuinely interested in them, so it was not too difficult to do well on the market.

Having sold another outrageous hat, I turned back to the gentleman as he was still watching me intently.

"Obviously you enjoy what you do Mademoiselle, and you do it very well, I might add," he said. His eyes were crystal blue, Azure blue, like the sea.

"I can see that your creations are a reflection of you," he added. "You are a very wild, passionate creature," he paused, watching my reaction.

"I have a proposal for you, a business proposal... I would like to buy some of your creativity, some of your wild, abundant energy, but not in the form you are offering here tonight. I am willing to pay for a small portion of your passionate energy, which is basically what all your customers are searching for. However, I do not need a pair of shorts or a hat, but invite you out for the evening so we can savor the moonlight, a little wine and the view over the sea and maybe I can taste the fruits of your passion..."

Well! I had never received that kind of a proposition before, yet in essence he was right. Here I was, selling a part of myself I had creatively presented as colorful clothing. What was the difference if I sold a pair of shorts to this man, or charged him a fair price for some of my other creative juices? He was certainly attractive. His well-tailored suit sat across broad shoulders. His tanned, immaculately shaved face had an air of experience of life. He could have anything he desired – money seemed to be of no issue to him.

As if he were reading my thoughts, he added, "You will be generously compensated for your time and energy should you choose to join me this beautiful summer's eve." How could I resist? I had dreamed of being whisked away into the moonlight by a rich, good-looking Frenchman and here he was not only offering an experience I had dreamed of, but monetary compensation for my creative talents also!

Packing up my things long before the market was due to close for the day, I arranged to meet him in about twenty minutes or so at the café Veronique (a very classy joint), overlooking the sea. Taking my things to my van, I quickly undressed and slipped onto my naked body a sexy low cut dress that I had been saving for a special occasion. Walking towards the café, pantiless and braless, with my sexy dress on, I felt like the 'cat that got the cream.'

Good going girl! I congratulated myself. This is what life is all about! Taking opportunities when they are offered and enjoying each new experience. I had always wanted to be wined and dined in an expensive French restaurant, and then walk the boulevard by moonlight. Now I felt like one of the rich and famous that normally I would be trying to seduce into buying something they really did not need. Instead, I was now selling something this man obviously desired and I was enjoying the thrill and glamour of the French Cote d'Azur by moonlight.

As I waltzed into the chic café, where only the very rich and famous could afford to dine, I felt his gaze on me before I even met his eyes. He was very pleasantly surprised to see me looking so sexy and divine. He stood up, like a true gentleman, kissed me on both cheeks and slid the chair next to him beneath me.

"Enchante," I purred. I felt like the Duchess herself! I played the role of the mistress so well. Slipping off my heels I seductively played with his feet beneath the table. Each mouthful of food I sensuously savored, intimating that my lips enjoyed every sensation that came their way. I let my hand slide beneath the low over-hanging tablecloth and caressed his thigh, subtlely making my way up to his crotch. He was enjoying my teasing and responded proudly by flexing his private parts with mastery, indicating he was able to meet any expectations I had!

The dessert was the ultimate – a rich, creamy chocolate mousse. Enough to send anyone through the roof! I took a spoonful and fed him slowly, teasing him by sliding the spoon in and out of his lips. I took a fresh strawberry and sucked on it, pursing my lips. He was clearly aroused and obviously enjoying my flow of energy. He ordered another bottle of champagne – Dom Perion – and invited me out onto the balcony to enjoy the moonlit view. We made our way outside, a glass of the very best champagne in our hands.

As I stepped into the moonlight I gasped at the beauty of it reflected on the sea. There was a soft, cool sea breeze that was enough to harden my nipples. They stood out quite prominently from beneath my thin dress and my companion could not resist reaching over and placing his arm around my shoulder, allowing his fingers to slowly move down and brush over my very erect bra-less nipples.

Soft, romantic music was playing in the background. He invited me to dance with him beneath the moonlight. We placed our glasses on the table nearby, and moving into his arms, our bodies came softly together. The champagne sensitized each gentle caress as we danced.

Pausing for another drink, I asked him if he would like to try a new way of drinking champagne, to which he nodded affirmatively. I reached for my glass and took a sip. Holding eye contact with him, I then pressed my lips to his, slowly expressing the liquid from my mouth into his. It is such a sensuous way to drink with someone. I made it last a long time as I savored the feeling of his soft, yielding lips responding to my own. My passions aroused, I let go into the moment and once again became lost into the ocean of ecstasy, with the waves gently lapping the shores.

To kiss. Such a simple act yet its effect so profound. The reality being that when one kisses, two major meridians (energy circuits) of each person connect with the other and create a very powerful energy connection. If the fire is lit by a kiss, it is a very good indication that the rest of the pieces will fit together also. I was excited. I felt like I was in a dream, or a movie. Here I was having a beautiful evening for which I would bear no cost, au contraire – that I would be paid for! What a treat! And the guy was a great kisser too! This is not too bad at all, I thought. The kiss lasted a long time. It truly was a long, passionate, full-tongued French kiss. The kind you imagine the French famous for.

In his soft, sexy voice my companion whispered in my ear how much he was enjoying his evening and how he was savoring every mouthful of me. My juices were in full flow now. The good food, wine, moonlight, romantic music piped out onto the balcony, and a sexy, French lover to be with - there was a heaven afterall!

He motioned to the waiter, who was standing inconspicuously just inside the door, and a limo was ordered. All right! My first limo ride! What fun! And what a turn on. I always wondered what it was like in a limo. It seemed like there would be so much space from the outside. I was not disappointed – it was luxurious. The seats plush and soft like a deluxe sofa! He asked to be driven to St. Tropez.

As we settled into the back seat my hand slid up his thigh and again was delighted to find such a responsive man. I was over the moon and feeling the effects of the champagne. Without any regard for the chauffeur, I knelt down on the floor in front of the monsieur who was escorting me to his holiday mansion and seductively undid his trousers, caressing his beautiful member until it stood erect in my hands. I leaned forward and wrapped my lips around it, enjoying its texture and taste. I became absorbed by it, playing with it, deep throating it and caressing it with my tongue. It responded to my tempting, yet the monsieur masterfully withstrained himself, enjoying the sensations and making me play even more. The chauffeur, of course, was perfectly schooled not to even blink an eyelid!

My pussy was on fire. I thought to myself, how handy it was to have a dress on and no panties! I worked my way up onto the seat, lifting my dress enough to be able to spread my legs and slide onto my host's beautiful erect penis. Oooh! That felt sooooo goood!! I was enjoying this evening so much! What a great way to travel – by limo! So much space! His hands gently massaged my breasts and I slipped my arms out of my dress straps so he could suckle on my erect nipples as I slowly but firmly shafted him. Mmmmm! What a yummy feeling!

I glanced out of the back window and saw the moon reflecting on the sea. Then, my escort raised his head as if noticing familiar landmarks. He quietly said we would be arriving soon and that maybe I should cover my naked breasts and allow him to get his trousers on. Reluctantly I complied and he did up his trousers as we turned into a long tree-lined driveway. Quite a nice little holiday retreat, I thought to myself, as we approached a massive pillared house.

As we pulled up, the front door opened and a butler stood there waiting to receive us. Thanking the driver and tipping him generously, the monsieur took my arm and guided me into his home. Wow, was all I could say. My eyes marveled at the marble floors and crystal chandeliers. I was in awe! The view out of the windows was incredible – it was such a clear evening and the moonlight stretched for miles across the sea.

I was guided up a staircase and into the most luxurious master bedroom I had ever seen. A massive four-poster bed draped with chiffon, a jacuzzi on the balcony…. Far out! The monsieur came over to me and slid the shoulder straps of my dress off my shoulders and I let it fall to the ground. He bent down and removed my dress and shoes from my feet, then gracefully removed his suit. Naked he cut quite a figure, in fact, very fine indeed. Taking my hand, he headed for the jacuzzi. What a magical evening, I thought as we walked naked across the large bedroom and climbed into the hot tub. I felt as if I was in a fairy tale!

The warmth of the jacuzzi melted our bodies into one. Boundaries disappeared as we let go into the water and relaxed totally into each other and the moment. Inviting the warmth of the water to penetrate our depths, our cells responded with fiery passion. Emerging from the hot tub we collapsed onto the luxurious bed, lying closely to one another, our hands entwined, aware of our bodily sensations.

After some time, I gently rose and visited the bathroom. Next to the toilet was an array of different scented bottles of oils. I intuitively chose one and returned to my Frenchman lying so peacefully on his bed. I tipped some of the oil onto my hands and warmed it before gently rubbing it onto his torso. My hands glided smoothly over his entire body, sensuously massaging and touching each and every part of him.

The joy of human touch is beautiful. I loved exploring his curves and crevices. So rarely do we get to look at, touch and appreciate each other's bodies. For me each person is so unique, it is like discovering a new delight. The texture of the skin varies and each part of the body has its own quality. I spent hours gently exploring this beautiful man's body, using my own at times to arouse and sensitize his skin. He let go completely, surrendering to my skillful hands. My massage training came in handy after all, yet this was not how they taught us to touch. This was far more sensitive and sensual.

His body responded with erection after erection and he voiced his appreciation. Not one to pass up any opportunities, I graciously relieved the build up of his desires, first with my mouth then later with my juicy pussy – such a service I offered! Yet, as with anything I do, I did it with love and enjoyed every moment. That is the only way and of course, it is then mutually beneficial! My monsieur, drained of the last of his milky juices, drifted off into a blissful dreamstate as the moonlight shone brightly through the open window. I lay there in wonderment, giving thanks for the incredible opportunities that came my way and enjoying the luxury of my surroundings.

My gracious host had welcomed me into his home, into his jacuzzi, and eventually into his bed, where I gave myself full creative license to be as sensuous and sensual as humanly possible! He was certainly not at all disappointed and enjoyed my creativity immensely, rewarding me generously in the morning as I dressed, readying myself to go to the awaiting limo. A month's wages in one evening! Obviously he was happy with what he had scored and honored the energy and creative expression that I had put into the experience. An evening

I will definitely never forget!

Walking me to the limo he explained he was returning to Paris that day so he would not be able to see me again but gave me his card, saying if I was ever in Paris to give him a call. I accepted his hospitality with juicy, wet lips, making sure he would remember my taste as I slipped into the limo that would take me back to Nice.

Creativity is definitely a second chakra quality and I had now experienced the flow of creativity in sensual form, awakening totally that particular energy center. Such different love-making to my Australian or African experiences. I was high for days and sensitized to the max! I became totally aware of all the different smells and tastes and textures of everything I came in contact with. I was enjoying this sensory way of life that was a definite indication that my second chakra was alive and flowing!

CHAPTER FOUR

❤ *Second Chakra Activation in Jamaica* ❤

Color: Orange
Element: Water
Quality: Soft & Sensual
Music: Reggae
Activities: Sunrise, Fruity Massage, Waterfall
Physical Location: Reproductive Organs, Belly

I knew there was more to experience with the second chakra and I had heard the Jamaican people had an excellent connection to nature and fresh food. I found the Rastafarian men very attractive so I decided to make Jamaica my next destination.

The ecstasy of raw, fresh fruits I found to be absolutely orgasmic. Nature provided such wonderful gifts. To plunge my mouth around a fresh, succulent strawberry was heavenly, a peeled grape was extreme in its sensuousness, the juice of a fresh organic orange so quenching.

Jamaica abounded in fresh fruits and had its fair share of hunky-looking men too! I love to dance to all different types of reggae music so it did not take long for me to find a good dance venue with live music. Fitting right into the scene with my blond dreadlocks, I was welcomed as a sister into the brethren.

The women had a powerful presence and protectively looked over their men. I soon worked out who was 'taken' and who was not!!! And it did not take long for the young, single ones to make a move. I had my pick of about half a dozen stunning specimens. As per my African initiation, I utilized the music and dance to suss out which one I felt best suited me energetically.

These dudes were pretty cool about the whole mating thing. Laid back, most probably stoned out of their tree, there was no pressure, no hurry to make anything happen quickly. I could handle that! I was enjoying the good music and it felt great to be dancing again. I could feel the familiar energy surge through my cells as I slowly allowed my body to become one with the music. Reggae music encourages smooth, sensual, easy movements. Like a free-flowing stream, I felt nothing holding me back, I could relax into the moment and enjoy the steady rhythm.

I danced and danced until the sky turned orange and the morning sun began to rise. I went outside and watched in awe as the sky changed into its orange robes, softly greeting the new day as she awoke from the dark of the night. I felt the vibrancy of the orange sky enter my second chakra and ignite its glow.

Suddenly out of nowhere there appeared a banquet table of fruits that everyone partook of, giving thanks to Jah for the gifts. Such an array of color and aromas. I took my time smelling each individual piece of fruit, feeling its texture and tuning into its vibration. I started with a juicy piece of watermelon, then some honey melon, starfruit, a banana, finishing off with a mango. I felt completely satisfied and leaving some money in the basket, wandered off down to the beach to relax on the sand and let the sun's rays penetrate my well-danced body.

Taking off my sarong, I laid it on the sand and got comfortable by making a hollow for my buttocks. I strategically covered my pussy with a piece of my sarong, and drifted off into a deep sleep as the sun's rays deliciously warmed my naked body.

Awakened by a tingling sensation on my skin, like a soft, gentle touch, I opened my eyes wondering what on earth could be generating such a pleasurable feeling. Slowly my eyes focused to the bright sunlight and I saw the man I had danced most of the night away with, caressing my body with an orange feather. What a delightful way to be woken, I smiled to myself.

Continuing to touch me with his feather, he gently explored my belly button, between my legs and up the inside of my arms. I was in heaven! Then he reached over and teased my lips with a piece of mango that he slid seductively in and out of my mouth. He did not let me eat it, instead he proceeded to rub the mango over my naked breasts, followed by his tongue licking the juices off. What a turn on!

The texture of the mango was so silky and his tongue so warm and wet. He proceeded to rub mango between my now open legs and his tongue followed suit. I lay there in bliss, enjoying this royal treatment. It felt good to just lie there and receive. Gently he slid the sarong off my pussy and the mango found its way between its lips, followed once again by that sensual tongue.

My body twitched in glee as I surrendered to the sensation. His tongue was so soft and warm. I felt my juices starting to flow and the image of the fleshy mango the Frenchman had shown to me at the market, jumped into my mind. He was right. My pussy felt so fleshy and juicy, just like the mango.

My Jamaican mango man proceeded to move up past my belly, stopping briefly at my nipples before searching out my mouth. He placed a slice of mango between his teeth and slid it provocatively between my lips. Supporting his body off mine with his arms, he moved his smooth, sensual form between my parted legs. Lowering his pelvis, he slid his beautiful, hard penis into my waiting, wet vagina. The sensation of his penis entering me was pure ecstacy, filling my pussy as I opened to him, then gripping hard with my vaginal muscles as he withdrew, then releasing and opening again for the next slow, long shaft. The mango slipping in and out of my mouth at the same time as his penis slipped in and out of my pussy was heaven. It was divine! Mango morning massage and more! What a beautiful way to start the new day!

Blissfully lying on the beach, with the sun's rays bathing me in warmth, I felt my naked body tingle with the after-glow of my rolling orgasm. My pussy was so alive and sensitized after the thirty or forty minutes of slow, deep shafting. I was a woman well done, satisfied totally by my Rastafarian lover. The sensory delights of nature's gifts and the wonder of human interaction never ceases to amaze me. What a wonderful world it would be if everyone could stimulate and activate their different energy centers in such beautiful ways. Feeling no fear nor guilt, just simply surrendering to the moment, to the sensations, enjoying the gifts of life, these bodies, this existence and this earth. That is my wish for humanity, I thought, as I lay there feeling totally at peace within myself.

I had a VW Combie van that I was traveling around in whilst in Jamaica. I found a special spot in the mountains, that I called 'Paradise.' There, it was exquisitely quiet, totally recluse and removed from the hustle-bustle of life. It was there, in nature, that I recharged my batteries.

I loved being on my own. I loved the freedom of my independence. It is funny, never on all of my travels, did

I ever have any problems being a woman alone. Fear is a negative emotion that is often associated with the second chakra. By maintaining an active second chakra I feel this enabled my creative juices to flow. By not buying into any fear, but rather going with the flow (the watery element once again), I successfully began to enjoy my freedom to be me and express that in every moment.

I truly feel that if you are not exuding fear, you do not attract any harm. If you feel good within yourself then that is what you transmit and that is what you get back. So it is important to spend time with yourself, alone, appreciating your body and enjoying the sensuousness of self-touch. This helps create a healthy sense of self worth and security which then ripples out into daily life.

The sensuousness of nature never ceases to amaze me. The female form, the vulva, the curves, are all there. I discovered a rocky canyon and waterfall that became my nature retreat I ventured to each morning. The shapes the water had carved into the stone were the same as a woman's vagina. It was as if the water had caressed the earth and brought out her female form.

I loved lying in the vulvic earth moulds, with the water flowing around and over me, cleansing every pore. I took great delight in touching myself all over, feeling one with the feminine energy, loving every curve of my female form. I could touch myself for hours, exploring the depth of my vagina with my fingers, caressing my nipples, feeling the water move on by so softly and gently – kissing me as it passed. Such bliss!

The waterfall was orgasmic in itself. The feeling to immerse oneself totally and feel the water slide sensuously over the skin, was absolutely incredible. I could stand there for what seemed like an eternity, enjoying the sensual pleasures of the flesh. To lose oneself into the moment is a powerful meditation. Becoming one with nature serves to reconnect us to the greater whole. It gives perspective and offers so many lessons, if we only listen.

Here is a song I would sing as I partook in my nature feasts:

"I find my joy in the simple things that come from the earth. I find my joy in the sun that shines and the water that sings to me. Listen to the wind and listen to the water, hear what they say, singing Hey Ya, Hey Ya, Hey Ya, Hey Ya, Hey Ya, Hey Ya, Ho! Let us never forget, never forget, never forget to give thanks. Give thanks, give thanks, give thanks and praise."

Before finishing my self-touch ritual I would lovingly give thanks to my body, the nature surrounding me, and to the God force that created this wonderful existence. I am sure if we honored ourselves, the earth and this existence on a daily basis, we would receive more respect and honor in return.

CHAPTER FIVE

❤ *Third Chakra Activation in Germany* ❤

Color: Yellow
Element: Fire
Quality: Power & Passion
Music: Techno, Strong Classical
Activities: Authoritarian Anarchy,
Strength, Action, Vitality, Power Plays
Physical Location: Solar Plexus

"We've got the power!" the music screamed out into the night. After Jamaica I went to Germany. I flew into Berlin, found a hotel, dropped my things off then rushed straight over to the border crossing with East Germany where crowds had gathered. The talk was that the East German guards were going to let people come and go as they pleased. The wall was going to come down. My God, I was not going to miss this for anything, I thought, as I got closer.

Joining the throng of people I heard the loud speaker burst into life again. "The power to change the face of humanity! The power to fight for our freedom! To be free! To break down these walls that separate us from our brothers and sisters," came the voice through the loud speaker. I pushed my way through the milling masses towards the makeshift stage put together with packing cases and pellets, until I could see the guy talking with the loud speaker. He looked like a strong-willed, determined young man. The energy was starting to rise, the heat of the moment was taking hold of the people's passions, firing their intensity to make a difference, to do away with unnecessary barriers, walls of separation, to unite the people as one.

Fists thrust up into the air as the people yelled "Power to the people!" over and over again until it became chant-like. Here I was amidst a revolution, amidst an overthrow of tradition, pulled into the energy of the crowd, feeling the exhilaration and intensity of the moment. I could feel my power center becoming activated, the fire within that fuels our actions, that knows no limits, igniting.

Nothing is impossible, I thought. Years of tradition, of dictatorial control can be overthrown. If the energy is powerful enough it must succeed. When people unite together for a common cause, the energy of many is exponentially greater than the power of a few.

Becoming aware of my solar plexus which had

become tight and firm, I realized that my third chakra was responding to the power that was around me. It certainly is the emotional power center, I thought. At that moment I knew nothing could move me from where I was at, my power center had responded to the group energy and not even firearms, of which there were many, could have changed me. Yes! I thought, I could die for this cause if that meant freedom for the whole. The ideology of this worthy cause appealed to my deep sense of justice. My core belief was that there should be no borders, that we are all children of this universe, that we are all born on this planet and so it should be ours to explore and enjoy as and when we so choose.

I did not know anyone so I was alone in the emotionally charged throng, but I felt accepted, part of the group, I was one with them all, united in action, in determination to see the Berlin Wall fall. For too long now the people of the East had been treated harshly by the authorities, denied basic privileges, unfairly dealt with. How could this reality have existed for so long, I thought, an arbitrary line on which a wall had been built, separating Germany into two halves, separating the people into two totally different existences.

Berlin had so many outrageous, artistic, creative-looking people, so much vibrancy and expression compared to the restrained, fearful, plain, quiet people behind the wall. On the other side, any individuality was squashed, any attempts at expanding consciousness thwarted. Access to music was severely limited, books restricted to the classics. The young people of the East knew nothing of the luxuries of chocolate, sexually explicit movies, techno dances, ecstasy, self-empowerment movements, meditation, expressive art in the form of sculptures portraying the suppression of the human species, freedom to walk, dress, eat and speak what-so-ever you choose to.

Raised in an atmosphere of dictatorial domination and suppression, many knew no other reality - they lived, or rather "survived," in their own world. How will it be for them to arrive into this powerful, festive, determined atmosphere? I suppose they will get swept up into the energy just as I have been, I thought.

It was exhilarating! I felt invincible! People started to sing "We will, we will rock you, rock you" and as the pitch and intensity grew people started to push against the gates at the border control. "We will, we will rock you!" they screamed pushing and pushing, harder and harder. Everyone piled up onto each other, pushing the person in front of them so that it became a sea of people, an ocean of energy, pushing against this stupid wall that symbolized oppression, control, and authoritarian rule.

We pushed against the gates, we pushed against all the injustices, the inhumanities of the world that this wall represented. It was claustrophobic being in the crowd. If I had wanted to leave there was no way! I was pushing and being pushed at the same time. My body tightly pressing up against the person in front of me, the person behind me pressing even stronger against my back.

I could freak out, I thought. I realized I was powerless as an individual, yet I could surrender to the power of the greater whole and enjoy the experience. This is so symbolic of all the power struggles we find ourselves in, in life, I thought. We basically have two choices: freak out and panic or go with it, enjoy the sensation and feel the power of the moment. I decided to feel the intensity of the moment, the thrill of being part of something much greater than myself. Contributing to a force that would make history and change humanity.

I felt the heat rise, I was aware of my breasts pressing up against the woman in front of me and I could feel a strong man pushing hard up against me. It actually felt quite erotic to be sandwiched between two people, in their power, letting their emotions be expressed through every cell of their bodies. As my chest expanded with each gasp for breath, I felt the whole crowd take a breath.

I felt a deep connection with these two people between whom I was wedged. We pushed and pushed. As I pushed my body against the woman in front me, I felt my pussy pushing against her buttocks, and at the same time I could feel the forceful young man's pelvis pushing against by bottom. Wow! What a sensation!

The intensity of the noise was deafening – I realized I too, was contributing to the din. I thought of the Wall of Jericho and how it was sound that broke it down. The volume this crowd reached must affect these gates and the wall, even if it is concrete, I thought.

It felt like I was on fire. Everywhere around me were people, every one of them yelling and passionate in their power center, emitting the warrior cries. My body felt like it was burning up – the intensity was almost too much yet I knew there was no going back – I was strapped in for the whole ride! And what a ride!

I felt the man behind me thrusting with his pelvis, bringing his full force into each movement. There was such a power in his movement. It was different to anything I had ever experienced. Nothing like the pelvic thrust of the aborigine man or my African lover. Their's was more physical and raw, this had a determined power and strength behind it that could not be rivaled and definitely not challenged.

I felt the domino effect as my body was thrust against the woman in front of me who in turn thrust against the one in front of her. It became a pulse, a rhythm, a sexual energy with one purpose, one goal – break down the barriers so that everyone can be free. How symbolic, I thought, and what a powerful ripple effect this will have for humanity.

Somehow I could feel the man behind me getting turned on, his bulge pushing into me hardened and he started grunting "Ha! Ha!" thrusting even more forcefully. My body responded to this manly come-on and I was enjoying his powerful male energy thrusting me from behind. I reached my hands behind me and held his buttocks pulling him tighter and tighter towards me.

We were already incredibly close but that gesture was the "OK" for him to really let himself become aroused. One of his hands reached around and grabbed my breast and I placed my hand over his, encouraging him to squeeze and rub them. I had not even seen his face, but his energy was so powerful, so strong, it was really starting to light my fire. My pussy was getting red hot.

Somehow my hand found its way to his belt buckle and did a "Mr. Bean" maneuver, undoing it while being unable to see a thing. He picked up on my intention and leaving my breast, proceeded to undo his fly and squeeze his penis out of his trousers.

I thought, how lucky I was to have on a short skirt and no panties. It was certainly handy being a tall woman. I wiggled up my skirt exposing my bare bottom as I felt his penis make its way eagerly between my legs. I was able to lean forward onto the woman in front of me just enough so he could work his penis into my hot, steaming pussy. The feeling as it went in was amazing. We were so tightly pushed together that it accentuated my pussy's tightness and his size, which by the feel of it was very generous, thank goodness.

Once in, he grabbed my breasts again and not missing a beat, continued forcefully saying "HA! HA! HA!" He thrust his hard dick into me with each HA, and I opened my legs as much as possible and arched my butt back to assist him to get maximum penetration. I was going wild with desire and my pussy was drawing him in more and more as the crowd pushed harder and harder against the gates. This was something. What a feeling!

For some reason I remembered a really bad Australian joke (why do Aussies fuck sheep against a cliff? Answer - Because they push back harder!) and realized I was pushing back also. This was contrary to the aim of pushing the gates down so I stopped that and let the powerful male force shaft me deeper and deeper forward into the crowd. Folding my arms around the woman in front of me for support, I let my hands clutch her breasts. As I did so she wiggled her behind into my pussy, obviously enjoying it as much as I was.

All this powerful energy must be having some effect, I thought as I felt his shafting build and build as he thrust his penis harder and harder into my pussy. I was having rolling orgasms with each powerful thrust and I screamed in ecstasy, clutching and squeezing the breasts of woman in front of me as he shot his hot, milky juice into my welcoming pussy. Right as we climaxed the motion of the crowd seemed to give way. The gates burst open and the crowd surged forward and everyone collapsed upon each other.

Sprawling over one another in total chaos, I felt the elation and ecstasy of the jubilant crowd, aware that they had succeeded. Everyone started hugging and kissing. I had landed on the German woman in front of me and the man behind had fallen out of my pussy. The woman beneath me managed to turn over and we hugged each other passionately and started to kiss. Now that was a new experience! Kissing a woman!

She was a great kisser, powerful and full of passion, not holding back a bit. She grabbed my buttocks and pulled me towards her hot body, her breasts melting into mine. I became lost in her warm succulent lips, my tongue searching out hers. What power! What passion this woman had and she was not afraid to show it! What a turn on!

I could feel my pussy juices, mixed with with hot come, running down my legs, so warm and wet. She reached down and put her hand between my legs discovering me wet, juicy and pantiless. Excited, her hand made its way to my pussy and sliding first one finger in, then with the next stroke, two, then three, she shafted me with her three fingers, in and out, in and out. My very juicy and responsive pussy orgasmed on the spot.

Unbelievably turned on and wild with passion, I thrust my hand down her trousers and getting my fingers underneath the elastic at the top of her panties, I fingered her clitoris until her juices flowed. She had an incredible pussy to touch and as I continued to finger her, she also started to orgasm. We both came and came, fingering and tongue-kissing each other into mind-blowing orgasm after mind-blowing orgasm. My God, women know how women like to be touched.

German women seem to be so much more enlightened sexually – nowhere else in the world had I experienced this openness amongst women and I was enjoying it. It is such a shame 'women loving women' is not accepted by mainstream society, and is looked on as weird. It is so natural, beautiful and yummy. Such a turn on!

There is something so easy about loving another woman. There is no power play, there is a mutual understanding of what each other's needs are, there is a softness inherent in the strong fingers and a strength in those soft, wet lips. Every woman should experience loving another women at least one time in their lives, and hopefully many more – it is too good to miss out on.

Suddenly the loud speakers started to play up-beat celebration music, people started to pick themselves off the ground and it turned into one big ecstasy party. The music blaring across the thousands of people that had gathered, the bodies becoming one with the rhythm of the music, people dancing and holding each other, kissing, laughing, crying, celebrating their freedom.

Amidst the crowd I saw some new faces, obviously Eastern European in their dress, their expressions of awe and wonderment giving their roots away. They soon were welcomed into the crowd, hugged, kissed and congratulated. Imagine coming from a culture where music was basically outlawed, or at least severely restricted, a place where outrageousness was pretty much non-existent and arriving into Berlin, the most craziest, zaniest, over-the-top place in the world, to a techno dance party in full swing on the streets!

I was so happy, so much in joy that I reveled in the music and danced and danced and danced the night away, hugging everyone I met, kissing anyone whose lips came my way – what freedom, what bliss! If only the world could be like this forever!

The music and dancing lasted the whole night. I was totally unaware of the time until I looked up and saw the yellow glow of the morning sky. As I noticed the sky changing color I looked for a high point around me from which I could watch the dawning of this very special day.

The wall was not far away and where the gate had been pushed down there were "steps" up to the top. I clambered my way up onto the broken gate then onto the wall via the steps and was able to make it to the top. There were several other people there and they graciously moved over to make room for me. I got comfortable and looked out towards the sky in the direction of the sun which was about to break through the horizon. For me this is a special time of day – a time to reflect on where I am and give thanks for the gifts that have come my way.

I sat there in silence as the sun lit up the sky like a ball of fire. I felt the warmth enter my soul and awaken within me my own fire, my solar plexus radiating like its own sun.

What a special moment, what an amazing dawning day, what an incredible night, what a powerful experience to have been a part of.

"Thank you sun, for your energy," I said to myself, "You simply are, and I just am - reflections of the universe, dewdrops in the ocean." The fire in my belly warmed my soul. My third chakra felt alive and empowered. I felt so happy to be me, to be here now and experience the liberation and freedom of this momentous occasion.

As I was sitting there meditating I felt another presence. I opened my eyes slowly and my gaze landed on a man sitting not far from me. He was dressed quite simply and plainly. He must be from the East, I thought. I smiled warmly at him and he responded with a grin just like a schoolboy's. He had an air of wonderment and innocence about him that was so refreshing.

I pointed towards East Germany and raised my eyebrows like when asking a question. He understood that I was wondering if he had come from the other side. He nodded. He moved closer and I took his hand and held it. We sat there looking towards the blue morning sky, our hands firmly clasped. It felt like I had made a new friend and this new friend was not about to let me go.

I felt my tummy rumbling so pointed to it and rubbed it indicating that I was hungry and gestured towards downtown Berlin, intimating that I wanted to go. He hesitated and then helped me get down, not letting my hand go for a second. He had decided he would leave the security of his perch, his last connection to his homeland, and venture off to explore this new realm.

I knew where there was a fresh fruit and vegetable market so made my way through the streams of people towards it. My friend was goggle-eyed and he looked at all the people in their crazy clothing. When we hit a street with shops, he was like a little child, dragging me slowly from one window to the next, his eyes getting bigger and bigger. Finally we rounded a corner and arrived at a local market that had a great selection of fresh fruits. It was such a joy to see his expression of wonderment. I do not think he had seen so many different kinds of fresh fruits in one place, ever!

I pointed to a grapefruit and raised my eyebrows, he nodded, so I paid for one, then I picked out a banana and then asked the fruit stall attendant to put one of each kind of fruit in the bag. I was going to treat this guy to Mother Nature's gifts so he could really understand what the West had to offer.

We wandered over to a grassy spot and sat down. I got my little pocketknife out of my fanny pack and cut the grapefruit open to reveal a soft, pink, juicy center. I cut it into four sections and lifted one to his lips. He thirstily sucked on the flesh extracting as much of the juice as he could while chewing on the fleshy part.

After finishing the grapefruit, I peeled the banana and slid it in and out of my mouth then teased his mouth with it, sliding it in and out in a similar fashion. We breakfasted on the fruits of the earth while sitting there in the middle of the square like two little kids. He was certainly childlike and there was something so innocent about this guy that was very attractive.

We spent the day wandering around Berlin. I took him to the art gallery, showed him some of the amazing sculptures around town, fed him chocolate and other yummy delights. He was like a kid in Disneyland, wide-eyed and excited by the different sights and sensations. People all around us were celebrating the falling of the wall in their own ways and there was an atmosphere of harmonious camaraderie.

It was nearing night-time and my energy was starting to dissipate a little. I invited my new friend to come back to my hotel with me where we could order in some warm food, a bottle of wine and relax in front of the fire. I always had candles with me so after arriving at my room I proceeded to light them and started the gas fire. He looked perplexed as the fire started instantaneously and it was difficult to explain that I had not just performed an act of magic!

I ordered in a pizza and bottle of red wine and we sat in front of the "fake" fire (a western invention!), devoured our pizza, sipping on the wine and relaxing into the moment. The warmth of the fire and the wine penetrated our weary bodies and after eating we lay down on the floor propped up by pillows. I had turned the radio onto the classical station and my friend indicated that this was his kind of music.

We lay back listening to the passion and power of the German classical music and I could tell my friend was feeling more and more at home. We held hands and watched the fire, becoming one with it. Slowly I allowed my fingers to explore his and felt the texture of his palms and worked my way around each finger noticing its length and width. I had heard that you could tell a lot about a man's anatomy by the shape and size of his hands and feet. This man's hands were strong and powerful, they had obviously done a lot of physical labor. His thick, long fingers indicated he was well endowed. I decided to check further…

I sat up and made my way to his feet. Propping myself against the sofa and resting his feet on a cushion in my lap I proceeded to remove his socks and stroke his feet. What beautiful feet, I thought. Such wonderful high arches, long and strong. This was certainly a man's man and I was enjoying exploring this part of his body, sensuously touching his skin, my fingers penetrating between his toes.

I lifted one foot to my lips and gently sucked on his big toe. I could feel him jolt a little at the sensation and noticed the bulge in his trousers start to grow. Hmmmm, I thought to myself, he is enjoying this. I became absorbed by his feet, licking and sucking each toe one at a time while softly stroking his lower leg beneath his trousers. Such soft body hair he had. His lower calf muscles were solid, so I gently massaged and relaxed them, then proceeded to reach further and further up his baggy trousers with one hand while seductively sucking his toes.

I glanced at his face and saw the most beautiful picture I have even seen – the expression of bliss and surrender was incredible. The classical music in the background relaxed him and he was clearly enjoying the sensuousness of my tongue exploring his toes and soft hands exploring his strong legs.

The fire and candles helped to create the atmosphere and I could sense him letting go and relaxing into the moment. My hand reached further and further until it came to some shorts. I slipped my hand beneath the shorts and made my way to the top of his leg where I discovered a large, hard, erect penis obviously sensitized by my touch. He let out a soft "Ahhh" as I stroked his penis.

Meanwhile I used my other hand to undo his buckle and zipper and maneuvered myself so I could slip my hand down his undershorts and play with his balls. Oh how I loved playing with such a responsive male! The whole scene was so wonderful, the candles, the fire, the wine bottle empty on the table.

I let my hand slide out from his trouser leg and slid it up under his shirt feeling his strong muscular torso. I like farm boys, I thought to myself – they always have such strong physiques. Then I gently pulled his hardened penis out of his trousers and slowly lowered my mouth over it. I could see him start a little at the sensation but he relaxed into it.

I became more aware of the music in the background and moved my mouth in rhythm to the symphony. As it grew in intensity so too did my movements and then when it subsided into a quieter moment I relaxed my intensity. I could feel my own body start to come on fire with passion. I loved candles, I loved fire and I loved passionate young men.

While one hand fondled his penis and my lips sucked passionately the end of it, I used my other hand to stimulate my own pussy, touching it just how I liked to be touched, fingering myself until my pussy juices started to flow.

The young man raised his buttocks and slipped his trousers down further so I could take more of his penis into my mouth. Oh, it tasted so sweet – like nectar from the Gods. I felt the music grow in intensity and I stimulated my pussy faster and faster feeling the reciprocal energy build in my young lover.

Holding his strong erect penis with one hand I lifted my skirt and slid my hot pussy completely onto him, devouring his manliness into the depths of my sex. I felt his body respond as he let out a little gasp. It felt so good to have him right in me and I bared down as hard as I could while rocking my pelvis back and forward. I felt his passions rise and his hands searched out my breasts. I pulled my clothes up over my head so he could caress my hot, naked body.

As I increased the intensity of the movements of my pussy, he opened his eyes wide and grabbed me tightly. He looked at me intensely and I held his gaze while lifting my pussy up right to the end of his penis before plunging him again, filling my pussy to its depth with his strong, beautiful penis. The music seemed to mirror our intensity and the crescendos built and built as our passions got higher and higher.

His fire within was definitely ignited and I could feel a powerful sense of maleness begin to surface. He grabbed me and swung me over onto my back. As if waking from a deep sleep he was now remembering who he was and the lion within awoke with a vengeance. He ripped off his shirt and managed to remove his trousers while maintaining his strong, intense shafting. I could almost sense him about to roar as the energy rose.

He forcefully shafted me deeper and deeper, holding

me tighter and tighter, breathing faster and faster. He looked obsessed and I gasped at the intensity that was being unleashed. He was such a pussycat lying there in front of the fire and now he was in full power, every cell of his body tight and controlled as he plunged me, lifting my legs higher and higher so he could penetrate deeper and deeper.

I felt like I was losing control and being taken over by an obsessed, sex-driven madman! What had I unleashed, I thought? Once again, it crossed my consciousness, that I could either freak out or go with it and enjoy this power play that seemed to be happening. I decided it was time to kick in my power center and shift roles from being the prey to being the stalker.

I managed to wrap my legs around his body and with my arms around his neck I was able to swing myself and push him off balance. We rolled onto our sides and it became a playful fight of who was strongest as we rolled and rolled around the floor, maintaining sexual contact. I rolled on top of him and grabbed his arms holding them back above his head. I jumped up on my haunches and forcefully pumped up and down on his penis, burying it into my pussy with each wild pump.

He resisted my handhold and managed to grab my wrists and raising his upper torso I admiringly noticed his muscles rippling as he tried to flip me over once again. It was exhilerating as we played roughly on the carpet. I could feel carpet burns on my knees but the intensity was such that it did not hurt. He grabbed my arms and twisted them behind my back flipping me over on to my stomach. I raised my knees so I could get up and as I did so I felt him penetrate me from behind. Ooh, he was a big boy! But it was sooo good.

I wiggled my hands free and grabbed hold of the sofa, somehow managing to pull myself up. He pushed me onto the sofa with his powerful thrusting and my knees welcomed the much-needed softness. I rolled over and he pinned me against the cushions and lunged after me again. This time I felt caught so I responded to his thrusting by lifting my pussy to meet his thrusting penis with every stroke. My God this was powerful sex.

Feeling my pussy start to become a bit raw with the physicalness and the length of our love making, I decided I had had enough. But I wanted to make him come so that this little power play could have a satisfying end. I squeezed my pussy muscles tightly around his penis, knowing the stimulation this action incurs, and thrust my pussy increasingly strongly, using my hands to squeeze his nipples.

In the background I was aware of the powerful classical music building up to its climax and built my own intensity in time with it. It was working, I could feel him getting closer and closer and instead of pulling back I pushed even harder. A part of me was turned on by this powerful overbearing strength, my pussy responded as he shot his lot in one final, massive plunge into me. I climaxed by orgasming with him. He collapsed down onto me, totally exhausted and spent.

In a way I was glad that it had come to an end. It was almost a little too intense, almost bordering on physical oppression yet my body was on fire with the power of the physical activity, my pussy was oozing and dripping our juices and I was out of breath with the exertion.

As I extracted my body from under him my young East German friend collapsed onto the sofa and fortunately a softer more calming piece of classical music played from the radio. Wow! I thought, he really responded to that powerful, strong, passionate classical music that came on air! Somehow it unleashed this man's power animal which was a very strong lion and fortunately I was an equally powerful female tigress that could match this ferocious being! I would not like to encounter this animal if I were feeling at all weak or vulnerable, I thought!

Phew! This is truly the power of the third chakra and this energy can obviously be used to achieve whatsoever we desire in life, if it is activated. Now I started to see the importance of activating all the energy centers and not just one, so that this extremely powerful energy could be directed into worthy causes. This guy was a powerhouse – if he consciously used his energy to manifest his heart's desires he could move mountains and single handedly push down the Berlin Wall! This was the energy Hitler must have tapped into. Imagine if this power center could be governed by the heart, I pondered while lying on the floor, feeling my body on fire, what we could achieve in this lifetime would be phenomenal.

My East German guest lay back on the sofa exhausted and I reached for a blanket and covered us both as we lay spread-eagled, spent from the exertion of such powerful loving. I was grateful to have had the opportunity to really feel the power within me awaken and respond forcefully to counterbalance a strong, male energy. However, I realized once was enough for the moment and resolved to thank my friend for the incredible evening but take my leave of him the next day.

This was certainly an activation of my power center, yet the power activated felt more like control or be controlled. Interesting to experience but not one of my favorite chakra expressions, I thought to myself. After this intense episode I yearned for some gentle, safe energy to permeate my being.

CHAPTER SIX

❤ *Fourth Chakra Activation in Ireland* ❤

Color: Green
Element: Air
Quality: Lightness & Freedom
Music: Celtic Music, Love Songs
Activities: Horse Riding, Dancing Lightly
Physical Location: Heart, Chest Area

I had always wanted to visit my ancestral roots in Ireland, so that was the next country on my list. The Irish are famous for their green rolling hills, Celtic dance music and nature spirits. Their ability to see the positive in everything blew me away. The Irish are definitely heart-centered people.

It was a cloudy, overcast day in the town of Dingle, on the west coast of Ireland. I was out walking along the beach and made a passing comment to a man walking his dog. "So, when can we expect summer to arrive?" I asked.

His honest look of surprise made me smile, as he said in a lovely lilting Irish accent, "Well to be sure this is the best day we've had in a long time - at least it isn't raining." He laughed as he saw my expression and with a twinkle in his eyes, proceeded to take off all his clothes and jumped, buck-naked into the sea!

"Why don't you come and join me, lassie?" he called out to me as he frolicked amidst the waves. I shook my head in disbelief, but his joviality made me smile.

To be sure, it is a lovely day, I thought to myself. It really is simply a matter of perspective, how you view your life's circumstances, I reflected. So many people complain about life even though on the surface it looks like they have it made, and then there are those who seemingly have very little to be happy about, yet radiate an inner joy that is contagious to all who they come in contact with. The Irish certainly had a way with them that warmed the heart, even on a cloudy, drizzly day. I waved him goodbye, shaking my head, and wandered off down the beach.

For me, the beach is a sacred place, walking on the sand with the ocean's symphony playing in my ears, is a very special time. I love walking on the beach. I love to stretch my legs and feel my muscles working - must be the fire horse in me! The fresh ocean air always inspires me to open my chest and fill my lungs. I could feel my heart begin to expand as the air permeated my every breath, filling me up more and more with clean, fresh, pure air. As

I breathed deeper and deeper I felt my body expand and become one with the element of air. The air touched my hair and blew it behind me. With each breath I could feel my feet get lighter until it felt as if I were riding the wind as it carried me effortlessly along the beach.

I was so much in my own energy that I got quite a surprise when I sensed that I was not alone. I felt a male energy coming up behind and turned to see the man with the twinkle in his eyes, chasing his dog up the beach, darting to and fro like a little kid.

"So, how ya be there?" he panted as he caught up with me. "You're quite the speedy walker aren't you! Haven't seen you down here before, are you visiting?" - his green eyes searched out my own. He was a chatty one, I thought to myself, but I liked the lightness of his being. Such a change from the heaviness of Europe.

"Yes, I'm checking out my roots," I replied. "My grandfather was born here and I've always loved Irish music, so I thought I'd come and find out if it was true about what they said about the Irish folk."

"And what is it they say about the Irish?" he smiled inquisitively.

"That you've all got silky smooth tongues and could talk anyone into anything," I laughed, my own green eyes twinkling in delight.

"Well, I don't know about that, but they do say we have a way with us that's unique, that's for sure." We continued chatting away as we walked along the beach, then made our way up a track and onto the green, rolling hills behind.

"That's my house up yonder," he commented as we got to the rise. There before us was a quaint old-fashioned thatched-roofed house, with a little flower garden in front and two beautiful horses stretching their limbs out in the paddock behind. They heard us coming and ran up to the fence to greet us.

"So you like horses do you?" he asked, as I reached out to stroke the nose of the black beauty.

Of course, it is every girl's fantasy to ride horses and I had been blessed as a child to have spent many weekends hanging out at horse-clubs. However, it had been many years since I had ridden but the idea of it was still very alluring.

"How can one not adore such beautiful animals," I replied. "Their bodies are magnificent, the way they carry themselves divine. How their legs stretch out in full gallop is a sight to behold," I responded as I caressed the beautiful specimen before me. "I love the feeling of the air rushing through my hair and the speed with which they effortlessly glide over the land - yes, I love horses," I smiled.

"Well, lets go for a ride then," my new friend spontaneously suggested.

I had no other plans for the afternoon so thought, why not! Not one to pass up any opportunity I readily agreed to the wonderful suggestion.

He said he knew of a sweet little Irish pub we could ride to and have some dinner at. So we saddled up and took off along the beach, in full gallop. Then we headed up into the hills and relaxed into a gentle walk enjoying the scenery, passing the time in small talk.

What a wonderful feeling to be back on a horse again. I could feel my clitoris rubbing against the saddle, and reminisced on the reason why so many young girls enjoy this feeling. I could feel myself becoming stimulated with each rhythmic step my horse took. I took my focus down to my pussy and visualized my clit standing erect. My juices started to flow.

It was so peaceful to meander leisurely through the dales and up the hills. I had no idea where we were but was enjoying the easy pace and relaxed approach to the day. Time did not seem to mean anything here - life was to be enjoyed. I could feel myself easing into the saddle, enjoying the sensation of clitoral stimulation. The pressures of city life and intensity of Europe started to lift. I felt my soul take a breath of appreciation for this moment and started to feel a lightness in my heart.

The continuous green of the rolling hills soothed my eyes and my companion's humor warmed the cockles of my heart.

"Would you like a wee dram?" he asked as he reached forward with a little hipflask of whiskey. "It's noon time and about time for some Irish medicinal water," he flashed a cheeky grin at me.

We paused and drank a wee bit, enjoying the scenery. Suddenly the sky darkened and there was a thunderburst followed by an intense downpour. We decided to make a dash for somewhere to shelter. There was a derelict-looking barn in the distance so we galloped full speed towards it. Enjoying the speed and the oneness with the elements, I arrived just behind him, exhilarated and excited. We jumped off and tied the horses up under some trees then went running into the barn to escape the downpour. Collapsing onto some hay bales, my friend offered me another drink and I sipped on the single malt enjoying the sensation as it fired me up inside.

He gathered me in his arms and started to sing the most beautiful love song that tore at my heartstrings. A ballad about a man who was searching for his longlost lover and how he had stumbled upon her one fine summer's day, playing at the water's edge, whilst the dog was out to play. My head rested on his chest and I could feel his heart pounding, the vibration of the song filled my ears. I felt so warm and safe in his arms. The sound of the rain on the tin roof soothed me and I relished the feeling of peacefulness I felt within.

He continued to hum as he started to gently caress my forehead with his fingertips. The softness of his touch was beautiful. So comfortable I felt, lying there, the smell of the hay wafting up to my nostrils, the warmth of the whiskey firing me up from within.

I relaxed and felt myself melt into his gentle caress. Lying there enjoying every sensation, it seemed like my heart opened and all my barriers disappeared. I lay there mesmerized by the love song he whispered in my ears. His gentleness was so comforting that I felt no resistance to his soft touches as he explored the outline of my face. I sensed him coming closer and opened my eyes slowly. I was looking straight into his green, green eyes and felt the warmth of his breath on my lips. He very gently touched my lips with his and I melted under the softness of them.

Lost in his warm, juicy lips I felt transported to another time, another place, perhaps it was another lifetime here in this foreign land that felt so much like home. I've been here before, I thought. This feels too comfortable for it to be the first time. I had a flash back to a time where I was strapped into a buxom tavern girl's dress, my boobs squished up by the tight, laced-up bodice, my skirt of many layers hanging heavy on my legs. The woolen trousers of my lover chaffed my legs as he rubbed himself against me. Celtic music, laughter and hilarity was the background noise and the familiar smell of whiskey on my lover's breath aroused me.

Was I dreaming? I wondered as I slowly opened my eyes again and focused on the man whose lips I was sensuously devouring. Uncanny, the feeling of déjà vu I was experiencing. He moved his body gently on top of mine and I could feel his hardened penis push up against my pussy. It felt good, there was no forcefulness, only a warmth as our hearts connected, the beat becoming one. Passionately we kissed and the whiskey started to work its magic, firing up our love juices and removing any inhibitions.

I felt my grandfather's energy come through - his words, "Feel your ancestry as you feel the whiskey merge with your soul. Whiskey is the blood of this land, feel it. Experience its fire, feel it ignite your passion, your heart. Surrender to it, let yourself be one with the heat of the moment...."

I felt myself letting go, enjoying the experience and freedom of being. The whiskey allowed me to enter into a very different reality. It not only loosened my tongue, which started to go crazy with liberation - exploring the depths of my Irishman's mouth, luxuriating on his luscious lips. It loosened my trousers, my thighs, my hips - everything started to let go and flow with warmth and a sensuousness and freedom only those who have been there before know.

I could feel myself tuning into my ancestry, into the passion of my ancestors, the fire that kept their zeal for life alight, that burned their rebellion against injustice, that fueled their fights for freedom. The heat of the moment warmed not only my loins but also my heart. A familiarity so deep, became my reality. I felt I had been here before

- this was not unfamiliar territory. Maybe there was some truth to this concept of past lives after all. Just maybe the reason I felt so comfortable with this Irishman I had just met was because in fact I knew him already. Perhaps I had been here before, in another time, another reality. It felt so normal, to be here in this barn, with this man. The effects of the whiskey tuned me into the essence of this land, this place, this experience.

Effortlessly my trousers slid down over my hips as his strong, warm hands searched my clitoris. My pussy was already wet and juicy from the horse ride, and my body was ready and wanting from the whiskey. He easily lifted my top and searched out my nipples arousing my passion to a forte. The smell of hay permeated the air as we rolled amidst it. The passion of the moment took hold as our bodies connected not only in flesh but in heart.

I felt his chest pound with excitement. The rhythm of the land pulsed through his pelvis, as he beat a rhythmical time, as if in keeping with an accompaniment of violins, percussion, and bass. It fueled my desire, and I felt my roots, my ancestry. It had an intensity and a speed that kept on driving, incessantly, rhythmically in time to the music of my soul. I felt it build in intensity as we climaxed, releasing a new surge of energy through my blood, a green, rolling, heart-filled energy that sent me rolling into waves of orgasmic body sensations that continued well after my lover was spent. It was as if the whiskey had set the ball rolling and that ball continued to roll and roll and roll, gathering momentum of its own as it galloped across the green pastureland.

I felt my heart expanding out as the waves of orgasm rippled on into the surrounding countryside. I imagined the sheep peacefully grazing on the hilltops suddenly feeling this rolling orgasm emanating from the barn, rippling out, reaching them, igniting within them a euphoria of being that sheep seem to exemplify. Then I visualized this rolling orgasm rippling out to the local village not far away. I saw its folk suddenly stop their bantering and feel a switch turning on, a remembrance of times gone by when they had experienced love. I could see their mannerisms change, the look in their eyes soften as the energy reached them. Their interactions affected by the energy of love as they carried on their daily tasks.

Yes, love is a powerful thing. Honoring and accepting that we are loving, sexual beings then allows that energy to flow on out into our communities. I truly feel that love is the fifth element, the key to solving the world's problems. Love is the magical component that is missing in the picture of life. It has been acknowledged through the ages as one of the most potent of all potions. It has been suppressed and denied by religions whose sole purpose is to control humanity and deny humans the experience of the beyond, in fear that we will all choose loving expression of ourselves, above the destruction of this life experience.

I felt myself expand out beyond my body, beyond the rustic barn within which I was having this experience, out into the environment that I was in, into the countryside of Ireland, into its villages, its communities and then on out into the rest of the world.

I felt my energy reach into all the countries and homes of the people I had met on my travels. My energy extended beyond my physical being on into infinity. I felt limitless, boundariless, expansive beyond the confines of the physical. What healing power this contains - the simple act of loving! Now I know why it has been suppressed - it is powerful beyond all imagination! It is the ultimate healing energy that we can all tap into because we all have bodies and can experience this reality.

However, I realize that this energetic reality is only available to those who are at a frequency that is compatible to it. I felt grateful and honored to be experiencing this sensation with this old soul connection, here in Ireland. I thought back to the loving I had experienced in Australia, Africa, France and in the Caribbean. Very different forms of loving that had served their purpose in awakening my lower chakras and enabling me to experience my physicality, my sensitivity, my connection to nature and the activation of my power center.

Here, now, I was in another country, Ireland, and experiencing a different sensation altogether while making love. It was a feeling of connection with my roots which felt very deep but at the same time, I felt an expansiveness that rippled out into the rest of the surrounding community. I was sure that the birds were happier in their song and the sun was starting to shine.

My head was resting on my lover's belly and it's rumbling reminded us both of the time of day - dinner time! The rain had stopped. We pulled ourselves up from the hay and dressed. Riding on up the valley, enjoying the smell of the fresh rain.

Not far away, we came across the quaintest little country pub. Entering it felt like a time warp. Beer was being swilled, banter was free-flowing, and in the corner were some instruments resting - awaiting human life-force to awaken their sleepy forms.

We ordered Guinness and the meal of the day - a hearty feed of roast and gravy. The sea air, galloping and frolicking in the hay had sparked a ravishing hunger within. I devoured my Irish home-cooked feast and downed my Guinness thirstily. I was enjoying sitting back and watching the scene before me, listening to the lilting Irish accents and far-fetched tales. Time seemed to stand still in this country. Folk were relaxed and easy within themselves. There was a comfortableness that permeated their every cell. An acceptance of who they are and where they belong that is rare to find in this modern world.

My friend ordered another round and motioned towards the musicians getting ready to start the evening festivities.

"These guys are great - you're going to enjoy this," he assured me. "That guy on the traditional Celtic drum is one of the best in the county," he said. "And the fiddle player is sure to make your toes tap!"

He was right about that! The drummer started with a simple rhythm, the banjo joined him, and then the fiddle added his unique flare. This Celtic style of music stimulated my soul and my feet responded by starting to move under the table. My new companion sensed my desires and invited me to join him on the dance floor. Well, you know me by now! Once I got going I could not stop!

We paused now and again to sip from the seemingly bottomless glasses of beer at our table. Time flew as our feet lightly touched the floor as we were swept away with the upbeat Celtic tunes. There was a strong drumbeat offered by the Celtic hand drum but the fiddle lifted the energy up off the ground. I felt a lightness in my heart that inspired my feet to step lightly on the floor - no wonder the traditional Irish dancers did lots of toe tapping and jumping around! You could not help but feel light on your feet with this music.

For me it is always fascinating to listen to the different music of the land and feel what happens in my body. The African tribal music really brought my energy down into my legs and connected me to the earth. The Caribbean style music really stimulated my hips into more flowing sensual movements. The techno music I danced to in Europe was really energetic and empowering - I felt it in my solar plexus and it really made me feel strong. And now here in Ireland I felt my feet lifting up off the floor and the joy enter my heart.

It was getting very late by the time we paused long enough to catch our breath.

"We probably should be heading back soon," my Irish lover drooled. "Don't you worry lass, it's full moon tonight so we should be able to find our way home, and if not the horses know the way," he assured me as I glanced at my watch. Midnight already and it only felt like minutes had passed! The timelessness of Ireland never ceases to amaze me. I felt dizzy with all the spinning and beer and was glad at the thought of fresh air filling my lungs, clearing out the toxic residue of the smoky Irish pub.

We thanked the musicians, said our farewells and headed off out into the night. The music followed us as we rode off into the moonlight. At least you can't lose your license riding a horse home, I thought. And even if I am not completely focused, the horses know where home is I could tell. They certainly were keen to get home - it had been a long day for them. They knew the countryside well and the thought of snuggling in for the night spurred them into a trot. The trot soon developed into a gallop and regardless of what I would have liked, the horses took on a determination of their own.

I thought - I could be a bit freaked out in this situation. Here I am riding a strange horse, in the middle of the night through a forest at full gallop and it really doesn't feel like I have any say in the matter at all. Even if I had wanted to stop my horse, I knew there was no way. I held on for dear life, ducking my head to avoid the branches.

All of a sudden a massive branch loomed before me - I let out a scream as I felt myself being knocked off my seat. I sensed Paddy behind me, also going at full tilt and realized if I fell from my perch I would be severely trampled. I felt myself swing below my horse's belly and as quickly as I experienced the sensation of falling, I experienced a feeling of weightlessness as my body effortlessly lifted back onto the saddle. It was the most bizarre sensation. Almost as if it were in slow motion, and I was outside of myself looking at the scene with amazement. It felt as if I had been willed back into my seat. I held on for dear life as we emerged from the trees and slowed to a halt.

I was shaking as I realized just how close I had come to experiencing hoofs all over my body! My friend had come up beside me and headed my horse off, grabbing the reins and slowing my horse to a stand still.

I looked over towards him with disbelief in my eyes - had this really happened? His expression confirmed what had taken place - he breathed a sigh of relief and he shared that he had seen what was about to happen and automatically visualized me safely back up in the saddle. It had worked! Love is powerful medicine and when passion is directed through the heart it can change realities, I thought.

Such a surreal experience that left me quite shaky. My friend Paddy, offered to climb onto my horse and hold me for the rest of the short trip back to his house. I relaxed into his arms and sobbed my release of tension as I realized just how close I had come to danger and how magical the escape was - I felt like the heroine rescued by the knight in shining armor!

By the time we arrived, my nerves had calmed somewhat and as I slid down from the horse, it felt good to feel the earth beneath my feet again.

"Quite a trip!" I commented as I was helped off my steed. "I don't think I will ever forget that ride," I managed to smile.

My Irish good-luck charm took my hand and lead me around the back of his home into his garden.

"I have a treat for you," he said. "It will help you to feel your connection to the earth again."

He had the most beautiful vegetable garden surrounded by the aroma of fresh herbs. The moon went behind a cloud and we were plunged into darkness.

"The reason my garden is so plentiful and healthy, is because I have a lot of help from my friends - the little people," he said as he took my hand and lead me up the garden path. "It's so easy to grow anything if you communicate with the nature spirits," he said. "If you close your eyes a little and soft focus, you may be able to see the little lights they emit from the top of their heads," he assured me.

I couldn't believe what I was hearing - here was this "Joe normal" guy, who drank whiskey and Guinness, a salt-of-the-earth type person, who was talking about fairies!

It took a few attempts to tune in to these little people, but slowly my eyes became accustomed to the darkness of the night. I started to realize that what I thought was my eyes playing tricks with me, was in fact the fire-fly-type light being emitted by the nature spirits. I became mesmerized by the whole experience, forgetting my freaky horse ride, as I became immersed in the life force of these little beings. I could sense their joy and wonderment with life and it became contagious. My fear and panic soon left my body as I allowed the joviality of my new friends to lift my spirit.

It felt like I was being surrounded by them as they sensed my openness and it was as if I were being given tiny kisses all over my body, as they frolicked and used my body and hair as a playground. What a sensory delight!

Well, the magic of the fairy folk certainly worked on me - I felt myself come back to life as I became totally present and aware of this other dimensional frequency. What fun! Paddy was a delight to be with and full of wonderful surprises. We sat on a swinging chair that was hanging off his balcony and I enjoyed being in his presence. He was so comfortable and warm to be with. He felt like a brother and I snuggled into his arms as we experienced the nature spirits busy at their work, playing in the moonlight, dancing to the music of the night.

This warmth of the heart connection is what the fourth chakra is all about, I thought. It's not about mad passionate lovemaking like my power center experienced in Germany, but rather a comfortable feeling of no expectations. It was more than the physical attraction it was in Africa - it seemed like a security of being that went deep into my soul. And it was not only a sensory delight like my mango men in France or the Caribbean, but a relaxed letting go into the moment that filled my senses completely. The timelessness of Ireland reached me in that moment. Not a care in the world or a thought about the future entered my mind - I was here and now, happy and present in the garden of the heart.

We made our way into Paddy's house and snuggled up together under the down covers on his bed. I savored the warmth and homeliness I felt and gave thanks for this very full day as I drifted off into the fairyland of my dreams.

I awoke early to the sound of birdsong and remembered the playfulness of the nature spirits I had connected with the night before. Like a little kid on Christmas morning, I eagerly got out of bed and traipsed out the back door into the garden.

The morning hues set a wonderful scene and I could just make out the little lights as the darkness disappeared into the light of the new day. I could certainly sense their presence and the joyfulness of the previous evening still permeated the air. There was a gentle breeze that tickled my skin. It was almost warm and I walked around to the front of the house. Facing east I awaited the dawning of the new day.

Feeling still connected to the playfulness of the nature spirits I was reveling in the feeling of the breeze playing with the fine hairs on my cheeks. With reckless abandon I ran down to the beach and tore off my clothes desiring to feel the air caress my body. It stimulated my nipples and I felt it kissing me tenderly as it brushed by, awakening my womanly juices. Oh, to be one with the wind - to feel it with my skin, gently finding its way into every crevice, touching my every curve. I abandoned myself to its caress and became one with the wind as it awakened my soul. My arms swayed like the branches of a tree as I danced with the sea breeze, watching the sunrise.

Then the thought of a warm snuggly bed brought me back to the chilliness of my morning ritual and after I had greeted the new day, I crept back into the warm embrace of my Irish lover treating him to a dawn breaker like he had never experienced before!

I spent a few glorious days with this remarkable man,

but as I tuned into my heart more and more, I discovered a longing. I knew it was associated with a knowing that there was yet more to be discovered. Although Paddy was a wonderful man, my soul knew there was more to be experienced. A yearning to discover all that I am seeped into my being.

Bidding my warm, cuddly Irish lover goodbye, I set off again on my travels.

CHAPTER SEVEN

❤ Fourth Chakra Activation in Egypt ❤

Color: Green
Element: Air
Quality: Lightness & Freedom
Music: Egyptian Love Songs
Activities: Honoring, Heart Connection
Physical Location: Heart, Chest Area

Since forever, it felt, I had been drawn to Egypt, to the great Pyramids and ancient tombs of magnificent times gone by. Back in London, I stumbled across a very cheap ticket to Cairo valid for three months. So that was my next destination.

My heart wide open from my experiences in Ireland, I was not prepared for the underhandedness that greeted me at 3am in the morning (the horrendous arrival time was the reason the ticket was so cheap). A man in a blue official-looking suit introduced himself as a government tourist official and guided me out of the airport and into an "official" taxi. A bit blurry-eyed from the trip, it took me a while to realize there were no inside handles on the doors of the car! Coming to with a start, I realized this was not an official taxi at all and that I did not like this scene in the slightest! I had a capsicum spray in my pocket which I grabbed in one hand and gathered up all my power.

"You let me out of this car right now or I will use this spray on you and you will never see again!" I spoke very strongly to the man in the driver's seat. I must have looked as if I meant business because he had such a shocked expression on his face as he got out of his seat and went around to open the door.

"My apologies madam, my car needs some repairs done, please do not report me to the airport, please madam!" I just grabbed my bags and took off in search of a real official taxi - one with signs all over it. Phew! That felt like a close call. I was so tired, I could not wait to get to a hotel, have a shower and sleep. Yet, although my next taxi was an official one, the taxi driver seemed to drive round and round in circles before arriving at a dilapidated hotel that he said was the only one open at this hour. I thought, screw this, this one will have to do for tonight - I will look for another one tomorrow.

The room was really skuzzy and yucky and there was only a sink in the dirty bathroom - I sponged off and laid my own silk sheet out over the bed and collapsed onto it in total exhaustion. No sooner had I closed my eyes than a loudspeaker blasted into action with the screechiest voice I have ever heard, singing "Allah.... Allah...." Obviously it was their call to prayer at 4 o'clock in the morning, and my window opened out onto the temple plaza!!! Great! I thought, as I stuck my fingers in my ears. What a wonderful welcome into Cairo, I cursed, Egypt is obviously not as romantic as I had dreamed!

The next day, jaded from lack of sleep, and sticky from the heat, I ventured into Cairo with my backpack. Stopping off at a café I realized I was the only woman there and was taken aback at the fact. Egyptian society nowadays is far removed from the matriarchal existence of times gone by.

A very good-looking Egyptian man came in and introduced himself as Ahmed. Asking if he could join me, I thought, why not - he is one of the most good-looking men I have ever seen, sure I don't mind him sitting at my table! His eyes were dark brown, his hair curly - he was certainly the sexiest man I'd ever met. He ordered a water pipe and the café attendant brought over the most beautiful, ornate vase-like structure that had burning coals on top and a tube extending out from it. That's how they smoke their tobacco here I thought innocently. He offered it to me and I puffed away, enjoying the cooling sensation of the water as the smoke bubbled through it before entering the tube. I started to feel a strange sensation come over me and looked at my friend queryingly.

"Pretty powerful tobacco!" I commented, and then he laughed.

"It's a mixture of tobacco and opium..." he said.

That was my introduction into the underworld of Cairo. An aspect of the heart chakra is the ability to trust. I decided that my Irish experience had centered me so totally in my heart that I was exuding trust and openness and that I would only invite those experiences to me that would serve me on my journey. Rather than deny myself this experience with this gorgeous, sexy, dark man, I decided to allow it to emerge and trust that I would not be harmed. I truly believe that if we come from our hearts yet keep our eyes open, no harm will come.

I didn't have anywhere to stay that night and Ahmed offered for me to stay at his place. Aware of what I could be getting myself into, I decided to go with the flow. We walked for what seemed miles through a maze of narrow, cobbled Cairo streets until we arrived at his apartment. His younger brother was there with another tourist from America. We all sat around and chatted for a while then realized it was getting dark and that none of us had eaten. Although they obviously did not have much money they insisted on going out and buying food for dinner. Myself and the other tourist stayed behind while they ventured out into the night. I took advantage of the shower and changed into some fresh clothes.

Sammie, the woman from America, had also just arrived in Egypt. She had met Mohammed at the bus station and he had invited her home. She looked very young and innocent and I thought to warn her about this whole scenario, but realized it was not my place to put fear into her so we just chatted about unimportant things like where she was from, her hobbies and interests. It made me realize how world-wise I had become and how incredible my life experiences had been so far. I felt so blessed and honored to have lived in so many different cultures.

Ahmed and Mohammed arrived back soon after with an incredible array of delectable Egyptian delights, stuffed peppers, falafels, eggplant, humus… YUM! I was hungry! I really appreciated them offering me a place to stay and introducing me to the taste delights of Cairo.

We chatted into the wee small hours and then it came time to sleep. It was pretty obvious that my room was the same as Ahmed's and that Sammie was going to share with Mohammed. We left the door slightly open and I could hear giggles coming from the other room. I went up to Ahmed and gave him a very warm, close hug and thanked him for his hospitality, saying that I felt the goodness of his heart and knew that he was a generous, sincere person. I honored him and I could see him respond. The slightly harsh exterior disappeared and he melted in my arms.

He was so divinely sexy with his curly, black hair, so different to his younger brother who looked more typically

Egyptian with close-cropped, dark, almost fuzzy hair and a trim beard. I really loved Ahmed's curls and purred into his ear that his hair really turned me on. His skin was the softest skin I had ever touched. I oohed and aahed as I explored his hairless chest beneath his shirt.

I whispered loving words into his ear as my hands explored his torso. I ventured down a bit further and discovered a very responsive male member. I gave honor to his maleness and he responded by growing even more. My pussy started to juice up, as it always does when faced with a passionate responsive man. I led the way, gently pushing him down on the bed.

Slowly I removed his shirt, and then his trousers and lovingly touched him all over, honoring his form, his penis, his skin, his hair, his smell. He responded by melting beneath my hands. I don't think he had ever experienced loving like this where the woman is the one who makes the advances and dominates the scene. I think, traditionally the women in Egypt are submissive and would never think to make the first move. He was obviously enjoying my approach. It was as if my attitude was changing any other ideas he may have had.

Still fully clothed I lifted my leg across his torso and straddled him, pushing my pussy down onto his crotch. I leaned down towards him and he lifted his head and nuzzled into my neck, placing gentle, loving little kisses up the side of my neck towards my earlobes. I tingled with the sensuousness of his soft, wet lips against my skin. He worked his way slowly around to the front of my throat kissing and licking the soft skin under my chin as he moved his head to the other side of my neck, treating my other ear to the warmth and wetness of his lips and searching tongue. Kissing, sucking and engulfing my ear with his mouth I shuddered in delight.

My hands clasping his cheeks, and running my fingers through his silky, smooth hair, playing with his curls with my fingers, I slowly moved my breasts from side to side on his bare chest. As our lips met with wide-open mouths, tongues exploring the depths of each other's throats, he slid his hands up under my top. Finding me bra-less, as I lifted my chest slightly off his, he clasped my two breasts in his hands.

His mouth was encased over my bottom lip, sucking it gently into his, I simultaneously sucked on the top of his lip. Our movements were slow, yet full of passion, gentle, yet with a sense of urgency. Our mouths continued to explore each other, our tongues never ceasing to adventure, our lips parting for an instantaneous second as he slid my top up over my head. Then we eagerly sought each other's lips again as I buried my bare breasts down onto that gorgeous male body. His hands moving over my back, soft, barely touching me, up and down, slipping in below the belt of my trousers at the back.

My body was in continual motion upon his, working

my pussy hard into his groin. Squeezing my breasts hard against his chest as we sucked each other's lips, tongued each other's tongues. He slid his hands up and cupped my head in his hands and then slowly slid his fingers down my cheeks to my neck. Our eyes opened and we became lost in each other's soul.

Not able to stand the sensation of my pussy being separated from his maleness by my jeans, I lifted my butt off his body, slipped my hands between us, undid my belt and popped the dome on my jeans. I pushed the zip down with my thumb and as I brought my legs together on top of his, he slid my jeans down over my butt. I helped him by wiggling and pushing them down over my hips. He grabbed the legs of my jeans with his feet and pulled them down off my body. I assisted him by pushing them off with my feet then playfully touched my naked feet against his, exploring his toes with my toes, enjoying the sensation of his skin against mine.

His strong hands gripped me around my rib cage and lifted me slightly above his body as he pulled my body towards his head and tongued one nipple and then the other, moving up under my arms, kissing the side of my rib cage, moving up to my armpits, kissing and licking me there too - the softness of his lips and movement of his tongue sending shivers of ecstasy through me.

He was soft and gentle, searching and seeking, every fold in my body, every contour. He lowered me down and our lips once again met. Wide, open mouths, we breathed into each other, savoring the essence of each other's soul.

The level of arousal within me was profound but I did not feel like madly burying his member in my pulsating, juicy, pussy. I was just loving this connection, this caressing of every part of my body with his tongue and his lips and his murmurs. "Ma Habibi," he purred as the tape of a famous Egyptian woman singer sang the same words in the background. Her voice was so sexy, her words sending shivers down my spine. He murmured the same words into my ears and I melted into him. I did not want it to stop. In fact, I was aching for more as every time our heads came close to each other, I eagerly sought out his lips and tongue and tongued him wildly back.

This was not ordinary kissing, this was wide-open mouths, breathing, panting, holding, moving. I couldn't hold myself back any longer and half rolled off him as I returned the favor of kissing his body, licking him, nuzzling his neck with my lips and my tongue. An incredible feeling of urgency was in both of us, but our pace was gentle, meaningful, deep. He kissed my eyes, my nose, my ears again and I returned the delicacy.

My nipples were ripe, hard almost to the point of being uncomfortable as his tongue searched them out again. His mouth opened wide and gently sucked my breast into the warmth of his heart. I arched my back and pushed my bosom hard against his mouth.

We were a two-piece ensemble constantly moving our bodies. Every cell was an instrument, the conductor was passion, desire, and the music was like a building crescendo, coming and going in waves, as our intensity built. His tongue searched out my belly button as I slowly rubbed my hands over his back, slightly squeezing his hard muscles, just exploring every ripple and movement of his body in motion. He moved his head down to my knees and slowly kissed up the inside of my thighs, one leg after the other.

My legs parted as if on automatic control and I lifted my bottom as the kisses and licking got closer to my pussy. Grabbing the back of his head with my hands, I buried his face into my goddessness. Reaching down with one hand, I grabbed hold of his incredibly hard penis and squeezed it. He groaned in delight as his tongue searched the innermost secret passages of my hot pussy.

Searching out my clitoris with his upper lip, he wide mouthed me as he sucked my juices from me. I twisted around and lifted his leg over my head so that we were in a 69 position. Holding his penis in one hand and cupping his balls in the other, I slowly kissed and caressed them. Sucking first one ball and then the other, gently in my mouth, and then breathing hot air on them.

Our bodies in constant motion, they moved and squiggled as he tongued my clitoris rapidly. I convulsed with pleasure as his hands slowly slid down the inside of my legs and I pulled my feet towards his seeking hands as my knees went into the air and he fingered my toes. As he once again open-mouthed my pussy, his tongue constantly sought out my pleasure spots around the edge of my pulsating vulva.

My God I was about to explode with wanton, orgasmic, desire. He withdrew his face from my pussy, lifted himself away from my body, grabbed me by the rib cage and rolled me over on top of him. Our bodies wet with sweat and passion, he slid his hands onto my hips and slowly eased my body down. My legs opened, pushing my pussy down onto his groin, that oh so beautiful cock went all the way home.

I threw my arms around his back, our lips came together in a full wide-mouthed, deep breathing embrace and I held on for dear life as in unison we ground our bodies together, forcing the very depth of my pussy onto the head of his cock. The shafting was slow, deep, but every cell of my body was alive, every cell was orgasmic.

My mind was a blur. All I could do was grip him tightly as both of our bodies drove to the depth of our passion. Rising to a crescendo within me I felt him stiffen and with one final thrust, the mother of all thrusts, our mouths wide open and locked together, our tongues intertwined, my arms wrapped around his back, his hands holding my head, we both orgasmed simultaneously, shuddering as the pulses of come squirted into me.

Waves of pure ecstasy rolled through my body. We lay there, still with our mouths locked together, breathing into each other, for what seemed like an eternity. He stayed rock hard and my pussy just gently pulsed and squeezed that beautiful cock, not wanting it to ever leave me.

My heart was bursting open. I could feel his breath go into me as I breathed his out breath in, I could feel his penis reaching up inside of me to my soul. Every cell in my body was open. Every cell in my body was welcoming. Every cell in my body was orgasming. There was now no sound, just the breath, as I slowly moved my hands up and down his back, gently squeezing the odd muscle, our mouths still locked together, my pussy still gripping his hard cock.

I knew in my heart that this is the way loving could be and I felt an opening within me, a longing that was set off by this incredible experience, to find the true essence of this type of loving – heart-centered, incredibly sensuous, culminating in a full body, orgasmic explosion.

I knew at the depths of my soul that one day I would find a lover who I could love on all levels, that we would be so compatible that every time we would come together, this is the experience we could have. I lay there, with my heart glowing inside of me. He shifted his weight and we lay side by side with his penis still gripped by my pussy, gently stroking and touching each other's bodies.

I knew that I had found another key in my search for my completeness. The opening of the heart was that key.

The opening of the heart opened every cell in my body, allowed every cell to feel the essence of love and loving and I realized that sex is way more than just a physical experience. Making love is about the soul and only when we touch that level of feeling within ourselves can we even start to understand the unbelievableness and the pure godliness of that level of connection.

What he experienced in my presence was pure bliss and his head could not have operated at any other level. It was the love and honor I transmitted to him that transformed the evening.

I left the following morning for Aswan and only later did I run into Sammie who had had quite the opposite experience. Mohammed had been very forceful and basically tried to have sex with her even though she did not want to go there. In her ignorance she had trusted him and he had stolen her traveler's checks while she was showering! She only realized later that day when she went to change money. I am sure Ahmed had originally planned to do the same thing with me but his well-laid plans had got diverted due to the altered state our loving placed him in.

So, coming from the heart did protect me in that situation. I was so immersed in loving and honoring him that that was the energy being emitted and that was what I received back. There was no way anything else could have occurred between us as the pure love was so overwhelming.

I am a firm believer that if you are completely centered in your own heart frequencies then that is what you transmit and that then is what you receive back.

I am reminded of the story of the small smoldering campfire. Along comes a wheelbarrow full of wet leaves (nasty customers like Mohammed) and the wet leaves snuff out the small smoldering campfire (Sammie's bad experience). However if, instead of a small smoldering campfire, it was a raging bonfire (like me!) then that same wheelbarrow full of wet leaves would become fuel for the fire (Ahmed's alterior motive was transformed by my fire). The closer that wheelbarrow full of wet leaves came, the greater the effect of the fire on the leaves until ultimately the leaves dry up and then feed the fire more (Ahmed melted in my love and fueled my passion further). So the key is to keep our bonfires burning so that any negativity that comes our way can be transformed by our energy. That is how I live my life. I honor every person, every being, every action, every experience. Learn from each and every one, but at the same time give thanks for the lessons learned.

Traveling with this awareness of energy meant that if I was able to stay in my heart and honor and accept everyone for who they were, then I had the most amazing experiences. People opened their doors, literally, to me. I was invited with open arms into families, homes, communities wherever I went. It was incredible! In Cairo, I was invited into a young woman's home, at the Pyramids a guy invited me to his place, in the desert I was welcomed into the home of a young artist, and en route to Aswan I was invited to a village where the whole community honored me with a feast!

I had always been fascinated by the ancient temples - the intricacy of the stonework, the carvings, the symbolism. There was a temple I had heard about that had been totally transplanted because the Egyptian government had decided to build a dam. Instead of flooding the temple they spent millions to work out a way of lifting it and relocating it above the waterline. I arrived by bus at the temple in the middle of the afternoon and was told that there had been a power outage and that the only way to see the inside of the temple was by lantern. How romantic, I thought, to walk through an unknown tomb with only the lantern's light showing the occasional encripture. The guide was very apologetic but I was enthralled! He said if I stayed the night that I could see the temple in all its lighted glory the following morning.

There was another tourist there who also wanted to stay until the next day. We both had sleeping bags with us so we decided to camp down by the lake, make a small fire and wait until sunrise. Out of the night came visitors with food and goodies to share. One was the local schoolteacher who taught English at the school and invited us for morning tea the following day. Another was a personal friend of the guard on duty and so we went up and looked at the tomb by moonlight.

The wind had started to come up down by the lake and I could see our friend talking with the guard. He came back to us, very excited and said the guard had agreed that we could sleep in Ramses office for the night so that it wouldn't be too windy. So, we gathered up our belongings and headed up to the temple.

Ramses office was the front open part of the temple, surrounded with Egyptian hieroglyphics, it was a bizarre scene. We said thank you and bid our friends goodnight. Snuggling into my sleeping bag I wondered how it would be sleeping in the shadows of such an ancient building... I drifted off to sleep with visuals of the ancient hieroglyphics dancing in my mind's eye.

My sleep was deep yet I felt so light. It was as if I was dancing with the Gods. All of a sudden I felt the presence of a beautiful white being with golden wings. She introduced herself as Isis and enveloped me in her wings. I melted into her and felt her heart reaching into my own. It was as if she were caressing the very depths of my being with her energy, touching me so deeply that I melted into her and became one with her. It felt like her golden feathers were gently caressing the inside of my soul, tenderly kissing every cell, loving them so totally that they could not help but smile and respond with love.

I felt bathed in her golden light. I felt her within me

and that little golden ball of her healing love grew and grew inside me. It kept expanding and flooding into every part of my body. I felt it flood through me, melting any pain, any resistance with love energy.

I knew that when she removed her wings that anything that needed healing would be healed, any old injuries, hurts, pains. What I did not expect, however, was that when the wings started to open that they would be my own arms not hers. She had gifted me her golden wings. To me that symbolized an initiation into the Isis healing energy. Whenever I would embrace somebody with my arms, with my heart, they would forever be touched at a very deep level. Little did I know that would be my gift to humanity in the future.

The heart is the most powerful healing energy there is. To touch someone with your heart is to connect at such a deep level, such a soul level, that the wounds of the heart begin to heal. The arms are an extension of that healing energy of the heart. To wrap someone in my arms is to connect at the heart level, to heal from the heart. There is no more powerful healing energy than that. The golden wings of Isis symbolized my entry into the dimension of heart healing, an ancient art taught by our ancestors.

I have spoken about past lives already. Sometimes when you meet someone it feels like you have known them before as I felt with Paddy in Ireland, and the same has happened to me with places. There are some places you visit for the first time, yet they feel so comfortable, so familiar that it is uncanny. It is in those moments that I know I have been there before. Egypt felt like that for me.

There in Ramses office I reconnected with an aspect of myself I had long forgotten but which felt so familiar, so real. Many times in Egypt I had that feeling, as do many others who visit that ancient land. It makes sense to me, from a feeling perspective, that past lives could well be a possibility. What other explanation could there be? I truly felt such a deep connection with Isis - the goddess of love and healing.

I realize now that I am Isis this lifetime. I heal from the heart, I am love and I love at such a deep level that it touches people forever. Thank you Isis for reminding me who I am.

In Egypt, I also became consciously aware that there was so much more to loving than just the sexual act itself. I was starting to see with my heart and realized that the heart-felt loving I had with Ahmed and the purity of love I had felt when seduced by Isis was what I wanted, was what I deserved. I knew that I could experience this type of connection and more with a very special person who was somewhere out there and that when the time was right I would meet that person and experience what it would feel like to connect with another on ALL levels and merge and be one with all that is.

I decided to continue my search, clearer now within

myself of who I was and what I wanted to manifest – I wanted to find the person with whom I could experience that multi orgasmic, total cellular ecstasy with every time we made love.

CHAPTER EIGHT

❤ *Fifth Chakra Activation in England* ❤

Color: Blue
Element: Sound
Quality: Expression & Vibration
Music: Chanting
Activities: Singing, Chanting, Trance Dancing
Physical Location: Throat Area, Neck

I flew back to England and on the plane met some twins who lived just out of London with their parents. Tim and Scott were about 20 years old, blued-eyed blond young men, very cute! We chatted the whole way back to England and when we arrived at the airport and they discovered I didn't have anywhere to stay, they insisted that I go back with them to their parents' place. Their Dad was there to pick them up and gave me a warm, welcome hug saying any friend of his sons was always welcome in their home. They lived in a very quiet town. We had tea and toast when we got in and shared our experiences with their Mum who was so sweet and welcoming.

I slept like a log and was woken up to the news that there was a fresh crop circle close by. The boys were already dressed and urged me to hurry up so that we could be the first to experience this new circle. We drove an hour into the English countryside; a light fog gently caressed the land and added a surreal quality to our early morning drive through the picture-perfect English landscape. I was still half asleep but excited to be about to experience a crop circle. I had heard so much about these mysterious geometrical shapes that suddenly appeared out of the middle of nowhere. Were they energy stamps on the earth from another dimension? Were they simply a hoax to attract media attention? What and who created these intricate forms, and what did they mean? All these questions buzzed around my head and we chatted deliriously while we headed to our destination.

We finally arrived and just as we pulled up we could see two people climbing the fence, leaving the field where the crop circle was meant to be. We rushed up to them excitedly asking them if it was true? Was there indeed a new crop circle? Did they think it was a real one? One of the people was the head of the crop circle national education group and she excitedly showed us an aerial photo taken just an hour earlier that showed the unique geometric form of this new circle. The man with her was holding a long metal rod which I knew was a dousing rod which measured the geometric earth frequencies of the land. He had an excited look on his face and said that this particular crop circle measured the highest response to his dousing he had ever had before.

"It's definitely a real one!" he said excitedly. "You'll feel it as soon as you walk in there. Have fun, but remember, be respectful." And they waved us goodbye.

The twins were both musicians. They were at university and on the weekends would play music on the streets of London or in the underground to get some extra money for traveling. One of the twins had brought his jambe with him (an Africa drum), and the other had his flute. They grabbed their instruments out of the car and we set off into the field.

It wasn't far into the field that we noticed just before us the typical flattened strands of wheat. We stopped dead in our tracks. It was almost as if there was a force field emanating from the circle. I bent down and studied the stems. They definitely hadn't been cut. It was as if each blade had be bent individually and placed in a particular pattern not harming the wheat plant in any way whatsoever.

We took a moment to center ourselves and give thanks for this wonderful opportunity to experience this unique energy then we tentatively stepped into the circle. We each went our own way and explored the geometric form. Each of us was drawn to a particular part of the pattern. Tim with his drum sat in the center of one of the large circles, closed his eyes and started playing a slow, steady beat. Scott found himself drawn to the edge of a key-like pattern at one end of the circle and stood facing inwards. He took his flute, placed it on his lips and allowed the energy to flow. It was a lilting eerie sound.

Aware of their presence but absorbed in my own experience I chose a small, tightly woven circle triangularly opposite the two lads. I stood with my feet firmly planted on the earth but could feel a dizzying surge of energy pulsating through my body. It was enough to keep my feet on the ground. Then I realized I didn't need to fight the feeling but rather go with it and allow the energy to flow through me. My body started swaying as the waves of energy pulsed. That old familiar fire in my groin awakened and I could feel myself coming alive. I tuned into the energy and allowed it to move me in whatever way it wanted.

My feet felt concreted into the earth and my upper body swayed like a tree, my arms its branches. I felt the energy surge through my energy centers, activating my lower chakras and then moving on up to my heart center. When it reached my heart center I felt a sudden warmth permeate my soul. It was as if I was bathed in soft, pink, cotton candy, but the energy didn't stop there. It continued up into my throat chakra. I could feel my chin lifting up, my jaw dropping open. My hands automatically started energetically freeing up the aura around my throat and I felt the cells opening. The energy surged through my body and I couldn't contain it any longer.

My lungs expanded and I let loose a shrill high angelic sound from somewhere deep within. "Hey… ya… Heya, hey, heya hey…." I sang. I felt possessed by some unseen force that was inspiring me to sing in a language I didn't know. I felt the vibrations of the sound tingling my throat, opening my lungs and filling the airwaves. My eyes closed, I allowed myself to be one with this energy and express it through my body and my voice. I became lost in the sound of my own body, immersed in its vibration.

I felt like I was in a trance. I could hear Scott's flute and Tim's drum and together we amplified the crop circle energy through music and sound - embodying it, breathing it, living it. I felt like I was on some very powerful mind altering drug. I felt so rooted into the earth but so free in my spirit. My arms felt like wings and I soared to limitless heights, my voice achieving sounds I had never before heard from myself or anyone else.

We must have stayed in this energy for quite some time, then almost as if on cue we all stopped. Slowly opening my eyes I made eye contact with both Tim and Scott and in silence we walked towards each other, every cell in my body tingling, with the vibration of the sound still ringing in my ears and on the airwaves.

We walked across the flattened wheat, consciously

aware of each step we took, until we connected in the center of the circle. We wrapped our arms around each other and said volumes with our eyes, but not a word was spoken. All of a sudden I felt my knees go weak. One of the twins sensed my fatigue and came around behind me and held me close. The other twin clasped me from the front and made an energy sandwich with me in the middle! We rocked gently and held each other, appreciating the moment, feeling our connection and the specialness of our experience together.

After some time each brother put an arm around me, picked up their instruments and escorted me out of the circle, back to the car. Phew! That was intense and definitely real! I had never experienced anything like that ever before in my life. We definitely didn't fabricate that energy reality. The energy in that circle was so real, so tangible, so otherworldly, it was incredible.

We were not far from Stonehenge so we drove there in silence and spent some time by ourselves with the rocks, grounding the energy. Then Tim said he knew of another rock formation circle that wasn't so popular, with fewer people, that wasn't far away. We decided to go there.

By this stage the sun had risen, the morning fog had lifted and we were blessed with a beautiful clear blue sky. Tim said that the place we were going to was an ancient fertility location where ceremonies were performed to honor the Gods and guarantee long life and lots of babies...

Great, I thought, this should be interesting!

The twins' Mum had packed them a picnic lunch so by the time we arrived at our destination it was time to satisfy these young lads appetites. We laid down a blanket and munched on good old English sandwiches and sipped on hot tea from the flask they had brought. Quite an intense morning to say the least, and the effects of the long travel and not much sleep were setting in.

It was a warm, sunny day and we all laid back on the blanket and stared up into the bluest of blue skies. I felt the warmth of the sun on my body and lay there lost in the vastness of the sky.

I love the English, I love their easy way of talking, their dry sense of humor. As we lay there the boys started telling me stories about the local landmark, the history of the stone formations and took me back into a time of long, long ago. They certainly didn't have any blockages in their throat chakras, these lads… they could talk and talk and talk, until the cows come home, and into the wee small hours of the night too.

We started to talk about their upbringing, their family, their parents and how taboo it was in England for parents to be naked in front of their children or display any type of sexual energy in front of the kids. Tim and Scott jokingly said they wondered if their parents ever had sex as they never heard anything, ever from their bedroom. We laughed, but it's a sad fact that in many societies sex is never talked about and if it happens, it happens behind closed doors, in the dark, under the covers with all noises stifled in fear of the children hearing!!!

I asked the boys if they had ever taken their clothes off in a public place before. They shook their heads. I pulled down my skirt and lifted off my top exposing my naked body to the sun. I said to them how wonderful it felt to feel the caress of the sun on my naked skin. They tentatively looked around to see if anyone was looking and then gingerly took their clothes off. Tim lay with his belly on the ground whereas Scott sat cross-legged on the blanket. It was a totally new experience for them both. I started to touch myself all over enjoying the warmth of the sun on my body.

"Go on," I said. "Touch yourself, enjoy the sun, feel it on your body."

Obviously keen to try new things, even if a bit tentative, they both laid down on their backs and started to touch themselves. Being young it didn't take much for them to get aroused, especially seeing me lovingly touch myself all over.

I said, "Break these patterns that ensnare you, get rid of the restricting chains that bind you, free yourself of your parents' inhibitions, become you, feel you, be all of you."

It was as if I were a channel through which this information was being presented. I opened my mouth and it started to flow.

Slowly I started to speak, "Close your eyes... relax, feel your skin...touch your face, your eyes... feel the outline of your nose, your jaw... gently touch your lips, run your hands down your neck to your chest, feel your nipples get hard as you gently squeeze them. Take a deep breath and on the out breath let your mouth open and say the sound Ahhh. With every breath make the sound as you breath out. Start making the sound louder and louder. Free up your throat chakra, change the pattern of silence, rub your belly in circles, gently, making the circles bigger and bigger until you brush past the head of your penis. But don't touch your penis... not yet," I paused and glanced over to see these two beautiful young men doing exactly as I told them.

"Raise your knees and run your hands down your legs as far as they can reach and then very slowly lightly stroke the inside of your thighs. Feel how soft the skin is there. Then work your way up to your balls, touch them, softly, squeeze them, play with them, and now gently stroke the shaft of your penis. Allow your touch to be more explorative, play with your penis, feel how strong and hard it is. Don't worry about anyone else watching. Don't give a damn. Be right here, now. And express what you are feeling, allow your breath to get stronger and deeper, make some noises... I want to hear groans," I said, increasing the volume of my voice.

"I want to hear moans, all the noises you have never

heard your parents make. MMMMmmm," I started to moan myself as I could see them playing with themselves, getting hard, stroking their young bodies, touching their cocks. The louder I expressed my joy and pleasure at pleasuring myself, the louder they allowed themselves to become.

"Work yourself into a frenzy, build up the energy, more and more... make yourself have the biggest, loudest orgasm you have ever experienced before in your life. Free yourself to express the joy of being sexual, alive, horny young men. Go for it!" I said.

I started to finger my pussy and got louder and louder as I worked myself into a state of orgasmic frenzy. I could hear the two boys moaning and groaning. I could feel their energy building. The twins were incredibly in tune with each other and it was fascinating to see them both build their orgasms in intensity and near their climax at the exactly the same time. It was such a turn on to watch these two young men, in their prime touching and loving themselves and expressing their pleasure out loud.

I could feel my body building to an incredible climax and held off orgasming totally until I could sense them both about to shoot their load.

"I want to hear your scream as you orgasm," I cried as my moans intensified. Then all of a sudden the deepest earth-moving sounds emanated from their mouths as they both came in unison. I couldn't stand it any longer and allowed myself to scream out loud as I orgasmed mightily with them.

"Wow!" I panted. "That was incredible!" They both opened their eyes and laughed out loud looking down at the mess they had made. Volumes of sticky white stuff all over their bellies.

"Waste not, want not," I said as I rolled over and licked the last droplets of come from Tim's penis.

"It tastes great!" I said, "You should try it!"

Tim tentatively put his finger into a sticky pool and raised it to his lips.

"Mmmm," he said, looking at his brother, 'Not bad!"

Scott, not wanting to be the odd one out, also scooped up some of the cream and tasted it.

"Not bad at all!" he smiled.

Luckily their Mum had put some paper towels in the picnic basket so I passed them a couple and they cleaned up.

"How about you?" Tim inquired, "What do you taste like?"

I dipped my finger inside my pussy and raised it to my lips sucking on it as if it were a penis, rolling my eyes and making sounds as if I were eating chocolate.

"Come and find out young Sir," I responded and Tim leapt at the chance, diving into my pussy juices, humming and hahing as if he were slurping up a fruit smoothie.

"You taste great!" he exclaimed.

"Let me have some too," his brother said, playfully pushing him aside so he could have a taste.

"Yummy! This is a great dessert," he said.

"And healthy too," quipped Tim, wiping his chin, "non-fattening, organic, straight from the source!"

We started laughing, good, old, deep belly laughs and we kept laughing and laughing and laughing. Whenever one would stop laughing, the other would start laughing at us laughing and start laughing again. We laughed so hard it brought tears to our eyes, which made us laugh even more. And then we saw an older man and woman walk by with a shocked look on their faces, seeing three naked young people picnicing at this sacred spot, and that just made us laugh more! We must have laughed for a good half hour then collapsed on the ground again staring up into the blue of the sky.

Freedom, the vastness of the blue sky symbolized freedom. Freedom to be whatever you want to be. Freedom to do whatever you want to do. Freedom to expand and fly freely with the wind. It felt so freeing to be lying there naked not worrying about people walking by. It was so liberating to break the patterns of our parents' silence when making love, even if just with yourself.

We all felt a lot lighter and a lot free-er when we left that magical spot and took a leisurely drive back to their parents' house. Over dinner that night the subject of taboos surrounding sex came up. As the wine flowed the conversation became looser and over several glasses of port after dinner we all sat around in the lounge and talked into the wee small hours about sex and sexuality.

Later that night as I was lying on my bed, I could swear I heard Tim and Scott's parents making love in the room across the hall. I was sure I could make out little moans and hear the odd squeak of the bedsprings. I strained my ears and sure enough, after about 10 minutes I heard Mr. Smith's very audible orgasm and little giggles from Mrs Smith.

Talking about things is very liberating and it sure seemed to free up the energy of that house. I wondered if Tim and Scott had heard them too, or were they sound asleep dreaming of screaming orgasms, their young hard cocks making balloons in the sheets.

I decided to go and see if they were still awake. I crept out of my room and walked along the corridor to Tim's room where sure enough the two brothers were sitting talking about the day's events.

"I just heard your parents making love," I shared, loving the look of disbelief in their eyes.

"True story," I said. "It made me so horny, I don't know what to do with myself!"

I looked at them both sitting there on the bed. I was standing there with a see-through shirt on. They could see the outline of my nipples and the shadow of my bush. I could tell they were wondering what they should do. I think they felt a little awkward, as they were brothers. Twins, sure, but still that's another taboo. Bonking in the same room as your sibling!

I said to them, "I'm so horny I think I need two hard men to satisfy me!"

Their eyes widened. Tim took the bull by the horns and said, "Well, why don't you lie down here and we'll pleasure you."

"Sure," I said undoing my shirt.

"I'll lick you," said Tim, "and Scott can suck your titties."

"Sounds good to me," said Scott.

So, I lay down and Tim proceeded to lick me vigorously while Scott suckled on my nipples. It was good. I started to get excited and began to make little moaning sounds.

"Uh oh," said Scott. "She's going to use her throat chakra again and wake up the whole house!"

"Maybe you should stick that hard thing in your pants in my mouth so I don't make so much noise," I suggested.

Scott willingly complied, unzipping his trousers and freeing his already hard cock.

I love young men, I thought to myself, they are always ready to go! And these two are so cool. They really want to experience all that life has to offer. They really must be indigo kids. They certainly came in ready for this experience called life. And it's so cool that they have each other to share these experiences with.

I devoured Scott's cock in my mouth and as Tim went to town on my pussy my sucking intensified. My moans were translated into a humming vibration on his cock which must have felt incredible. He obviously wasn't going to last long and looked a bit uncomfortable about his heightened state of arousal. I removed my mouth from his cock briefly and assured him that it was totally OK to come in my mouth and that I was sure there would be more where that came from.

Scott exploded like crazy into my hot mouth, shooting down my throat. I had no option but to swallow and the energy surge that flowed through my body from that young virile man was so intense that my pussy gushed all over Tim's face. He spluttered a little and I gasped for breath.

"I'm on fire!" I cried. "Tim! You'll have to help me out here," I said looking at him imploringly.

"My pussy needs a nice hard cock in it," I said.

Tim had already unbuttoned his jeans and pulled out his raging hard-on. I lay there on the bed with my legs spread wide open and slapped my pussy, saying "Here boy!" He climbed up onto the bed and humped me like a mad man. Scott's hard-on never went down. Even though he had exploded like crazy, he was so turned on by the scene that his cock stayed rock hard. Feeling the warmth of my pussy and my pussy muscles squeezing his cock, Tim didn't last long and exploded his load into me. He collapsed on the bed next to me.

I think the word for someone like me, an older woman seducing young lads, is a cougar. I definitely felt like one. I was so turned on. I grabbed Scott's still hard cock, squeezed it and smiled into his eyes, sticking my tongue down his throat. Then I turned around and presented my tight little butt to him. He slipped his raging hard on into my pussy and shafted me intensely. I could feel my urge to scream again rise and stuck Tim's cock in my mouth to quieten the intensity of my orgasms. This was phenomenal.

Women always complain about younger men firing their load too quickly, but the answer to that is to have two at once. As soon as one exploded I took advantage of the other one, and vice versa. I was in heaven. Here I was with two gorgeous young, virile, conscious men, in their prime and reveling in the fact that an outrageously sexy, horny woman was in their midst and loving their youthfulness.

Here's to you Mrs Robinson, I could hear them say in their heads. I think they must have come about three times each and me about a million times. Then we all collapsed on the bed in orgasmic bliss.

I thanked them both for helping me out and they responded in unison in gentlemanly fashion with "Our pleasure!"

We fell asleep spooning, with me in the middle and

by the break of dawn I awoke and gently removed myself and retreated into my room, least their parents walk in unannounced and find us all intertwined.

I really enjoyed spending time with that wonderful family but the call of distant lands beckoned me and I felt the urge to venture forth once again into lands unknown, in search of the "more" that I knew existed, that my soul was yearning for, to meet that special person with whom I could experience it ALL.

This time I headed off to Nepal, I wanted to feel that fresh mountain air permeate my lungs, feel the high of being right up on top of the world and explore what the East had to offer me on my journey of self discovery.

CHAPTER NINE

❤ *Fifth Chakra Activation in the Himalayas* ❤

Color: Blue
Element: Sound
Quality: Expression & Vibration
Music: Chanting, Overtoning
Activities: Singing, Chanting
Physical Location: Throat Area, Neck

I arrived in Kathmandu and was overwhelmed by the sights and sounds. The city bustled with people, cars, noise, smells, images, color and vibrancy. But coming from years of living in nature it all felt a bit much. I decided to take off into the mountains and see the real Nepal. The bus ride along the narrow, steep, unsealed roads was exhilarating but a bit scary at times.

When I finally arrived at the first town at the beginning of the Annapurna circuit I was exhausted. I found a guesthouse to stay in and collapsed on my bed, drifting off into a deep sleep. I didn't even have enough energy to take off my clothes.

In the middle of the night I subconsciously became aware of a distant screeching sound. Is it birds? I wondered, but thought it couldn't be because it was the middle of the night.

What is that sound? I thought as I lay there in this foreign land. I couldn't work it out and it got the better of me. I got up and draped a shawl around my shoulders and headed out into the night.

The village was dark and silent. No street lights or bustling motorcars here. I oriented myself and strained to hear where the noise was coming from. It was intermittent and almost sounded as if someone was blowing into a trumpet but didn't quite know how to play it properly. Traipsing through the dark streets, I followed the noise until I heard the muttering of voices. It was a monotonous chanting interspersed with screeching sounds I had heard earlier.

I found myself outside the local temple. The door was slightly ajar and I sneaked a look inside. One of the monks closest to the door motioned me to come inside and sit. I felt honored yet a little intrusive, but took up his invitation and tried to sit inconspicuously in the corner.

What I saw was fascinating. A room full of monks dressed in maroon-colored robes with yellow scarves around their necks mumbling some sort of chant incessantly. The screeching came from a crude-looking trumpet with tassels on it. This was obviously some sort of ritual and I felt blessed to have stumbled on it. I sat there in awe and felt bathed in the vibration of the chanting.

I closed my eyes and felt the waves of the sounds flowing through my body. I started to rock gently and once again that familiar feeling came over me. I've been here before, I thought. The haunting sounds filled my body and I started to transcend into an altered state. I could feel my throat light up and I found myself mumbling similar word sounds in rhythmic fashion. The vibration within and the vibration on the outside was intense. My cells started to tingle and my body heated up.

I felt a gentle hand on my shoulder and opened my eyes slowly to see a beautiful shaven-headed monk next to me. He proceeded to place one hand on my forehead and one hand on my heart and I felt an instant surge of energy followed by a dramatic feeling of calmness.

Wow, I thought, this is powerful stuff! I looked at the monk and nodded my head in appreciation as he rose and returned to his place. I sat there for a while longer gathering my senses and decided that I should head back to my room and rest. What an intense experience.

I stood up with some difficulty and removed myself as inconspicuously as I could. Out in the fresh air I took a deep breath and felt my lungs expand. I let out a long sigh and marveled at how blessed I was to have inadvertently come across this magical event.

Looking up I saw the biggest full moon you could ever imagine. I walked a little down the street and sat beneath a large, old banyan tree. I marveled at how perfect the moon was. It just simply existed. It just was. And I marveled at the tree I was resting by. It simply was there, happy being a tree. I marveled at me and the wonderful life I led, the experiences I had and the beauty of love I had shared. I simply was, me in all my radiance, just me. And the words of a song/chant came to me:

"Thank you moon, for your energy. You simply are, and I just am - reflections of the universe, dew drops in the ocean. Thank you moon, thank you air, thank you universe, thank you tree, thank you, thank you, thank you, thank me."

I went back to my room and lay on my bed giving thanks for the wonderful experience I had just had. Wow! Life is amazing! Thank you universe!

I awoke to the sounds of village people busy with their morning chores. I packed up my things, had a hot cup of tea and ventured forth on my way. As I walked to the outskirts of the town and towards the rice fields, I started to think about life in the West and how so many people become self-absorbed, worrying about unnecessary little things, governed by the pettiness of the daily grind.

Looking around me I could see such a different way of life. People were happy within themselves, happy with what they had (no matter how much or how little), they took time to sit and have a cup of tea and talk with their neighbors, they tended the fields and washed their clothes in the river.

There is a saying I heard from one wise monk in Kathmandu who was describing meditation. He called the thoughts in the mind clouds and that meditation was being able to sit and watch the clouds, witness the clouds but know that they too shall pass. It was profound to me and as I walked and climbed up towards the mountains I watched the clouds in the distance coming and going and realized that life's experiences are like clouds. We can either get caught up and lost in the clouds and lose sight of the blue skies behind, or we can witness them as just that, clouds. Temporary, always changing.

As I climbed in altitude I could feel my own energy getting lighter. The clouds became less and less and the sun got stronger and stronger. I turned around and looked down towards the valley I had just come from and turned around again and looked towards the mountains I was heading to. Life is like that, I philosophized. There are valleys and peaks, highs and lows, good experiences and not so good experiences. But as with all highs, all mountain peaks, they would not exist if there were not any valleys. So, too we would not appreciate the highs in our lives if we never had any lows. However I also felt that there was never really anything that could be considered a "bad" experience. It was all a matter of perception. They are simply experiences and it is how we choose to see them that is the important thing. I had had quite a few interesting experiences on my travels which could have been termed "bad" experiences, or potentially hazardous, but somehow I had chosen to put them in a positive light and see them simply as experiences.

The profoundness of this revelation hit me. I actually found the valleys in my life as orgasmic as the peaks. I suppose I was blessed with a positive attitude but in essence it really is a question of choice. It is the choices we make that determine the experiences we have and the attitude we take to those experiences that determine the lessons we gain.

I had been feeling tired and heavy and was thinking about many things in my head. I had been suffering from a headache for the last couple of days and as I climbed in altitude the headache was lessening. I started to hum a little tune to myself.

"Cloud watching, watching the clouds. Knowing that these too shall pass. Orgasmic valleys, rising peaks. It's good to feel the earth and my feet. Sun is shining, shining on me. Here I am and I feel free. Sun is shining, shining on me. This is what I call ecstasy."

It felt sooo good to be back in nature and this was nature at its best, pure and pristine. I decided to rest a little and made my way off the beaten track, climbing up onto a rocky outlay. I looked around and marveled at how wonderful it was to be alone and one with nature.

The sun was beating down on me and I couldn't help peeling off my clothes and lying sheltered between the rocks soaking up the sun's rays. I lay there and looked up into the blue sky. It's the most amazing feeling to allow yourself to merge with the immenseness of the sky and feel your limits and boundaries disappearing.

Stretching my arms wide I opened my mouth and toned Ahhhhhhh. Then closing my mouth the sound continued and transformed into an Ommmm. AhOm. I repeated this over and over enjoying the vibration of it as it flowed through my body.

All of a sudden, out of nowhere comes this voice, "Are you OK there?" I looked to my right and coming down the mountain with a backpack and walking stick was this lovely looking chap, with sandy brown hair and a long moustache, with a concerned look on his face.

"Are you OK?" he asked again, pausing on the crevice above me.

I suppose I must have looked a bit odd, lying there naked with my arms outstretched. Not the normal sight one would expect to see up in the Himalayas. Maybe he thought I had been attacked and raped and left there moaning in pain. I didn't think my toning was that bad, but laughed at the scene.

"I'm very fine, thank you," I responded, smiling.

"How are you?"

It was a strange angle to be looking at someone so I raised myself into a sitting position and draped my sarong around me so as not to make this man feel uncomfortable.

"I'm very good, thank you," he responded politely. "But may I ask what you are doing?" he asked with an incredulous tone in his voice.

"I was enjoying the gifts of nature and experimenting with some toning I heard in a temple last night – powerful stuff," I said.

"Yes, obviously," he quirked, looking me up and down, "Enough to drive someone barmy!"

I laughed at his English prudishness. "Why don't you sit for a while with me," I asked, "Or are you in a rush to get somewhere?"

I was being a little sarcastic and he understood that I was trying to take the mickey out of him and give him a hard time.

"Why thank you my dear," he responded and took off his backpack and sat down on a rock closer to me.

"May I introduce myself to you," he said extending his hand. "My name is James. I just bivied overnight at the base of that peak there and climbed her at sunrise," he said. "Absolutely spectacular! But my feet are hurting a bit with this downhill descent."

"Take your boots off and anything else you dare to, and rest a while," I smiled.

He sat down, took off his boots, unbuttoned his shirt and removed it to reveal a spectacular lean muscular body. His muscles rippled in the sun, sweat glistening on his skin.

"So, tell me," he said. "What's this toning you were doing?"

"It's an ancient chanting method used in many of the old cultures to awaken the throat chakra and open up the third eye. Have you never tried it? It's fabulous!"

He looked at me incredulously as if I must be mad.

"Now what would you be wanting to do that for, may I ask," he queried.

"Well. Have you ever wanted to experience more in life. To feel every cell in your body come alive and tingle and feel every part of your body, heart and soul activated to such an extreme that it feels like you are orgasming in every fiber of your being?" I looked at him intently.

"Well I've never really thought about that, but I suppose that could be interesting," he pondered. "How do you go about doing that then?" he asked.

I felt he genuinely was intrigued and so I decided to be quite forward.

"Would you allow me to sit on your lap?" I asked innocently.

I stood up, tied my sarong around my chest, lifted my leg over him and sat on his lap. "Oh my," he gasped as he saw my naked little bush fleetingly exposed.

"OK," I said. "Place one hand behind me at the base of my spine, and the other on the back between my shoulder blades, and I'll do the same to you."

As if he were a school kid being told what to do, he obeyed me gently placing his hands where I told him to.

"Now, rest your forehead against mine and take a deep breath. Close your eyes and feel the breath going in and out. On the next out breath, say 'Ah'," We both breathed and exhaled, saying "Ah" in unison. "Do you feel the vibration?" I asked and he nodded.

We did it again a couple of times and then I told him to close his lips after he says "Ah" and continue to hum the sound through his lips and feel the vibration.

"Can you feel the vibration on your lips?" I asked.

He nodded and we continued to breathe together and tone. The vibrations started to increase in my body and I could feel the heat starting to rise in his body too. I had never done toning like this before but it was fantastic! Double intensity.

Slowly I edged myself a little closer to him until our mouths were almost touching. I could feel his warm breath on my lips and the vibration of his toning. It was intense. I stopped toning and sat there feeling the energy flowing through my body. He stopped too and sat motionless obviously experiencing sensations he never had before.

Our lips were still touching and my throat felt a little dry from the toning. I moistened my lips with my tongue and brushed his lips as I did so. He did the same, his tongue gently brushing by my lips. Tentatively, as if kissing for the first time, our senses totally heightened by the vibrations of the toning, we connected our lips.

Pushing my pussy closer to him, I felt him respond. I reached down and undid his trousers, wiggling myself so that I could free his hard cock, yet maintain contact with his lips. I stroked it as I sat on his lap and managed to wiggle myself onto it so that it slipped into my juicy little pussy.

Feeling him inside me, our lips locked, we connected our hearts. I pulled him tight with my arms and started to hum. The vibration going through my lips, into his. Rocking forward and back as I continued to tone, was amazing. He responded by humming as well and soon we were rocking and toning and vibrating as one.

The intensity of the rocking continued to build as our breathing intensified and I could feel a kundalini surge beginning to rise through my spine. I couldn't hold his gaze any longer and closed my eyes feeling the shuddering orgasm vibrate through my spine. This was his cue to allow himself to let go too and he relaxed his grip, arched his back then crumpled forward as he came deep within my pussy. Shuddering with aftershocks we both jiggled like jelly.

It took a while for the jelly to settle and then we opened our eyes and let out a sigh.

"Wow!" he said, "I like that toning idea of yours!!! I've

never experienced anything quite like that before! Where are you headed from here? Up or down?" he asked.

"It's all up from here babe," I smiled and he laughed.

"I guess so! It would definitely be hard to repeat that experience!" he said, to which I responded,

"Well, we could have fun trying!"

I slipped off his cock and we repositioned ourselves on the rocks and enjoyed the sunshine until our tummies started to rumble.

"There's a great little chai house just up the way a bit. Would you like to join me for lunch?" he asked so politely.

"I'd be delighted!" I responded in the best proper English accent I could muster.

We tried the toning on several further occasions and it really did open up the throat chakra and other areas! After completing the Anapurna circuit we arrived down in Pokhara, a great little lakeside town bustling with tourists, places to eat, people to watch. It was here that I had an incredible eye-opening experience, especially of my third eye!

CHAPTER TEN

❤ *Sixth Chakra Activation in Nepal* ❤

Color: Indigo
Element: Ether
Quality: Insights & All-seeing
Music: Classical Music
Activities: Conscious Awareness,
Orchestrating Your Reality in Your Mind's Eye
Physical Location: Third Eye, Forehead

On the edge of Pokhara village I noticed that there always seemed to be some Tibetan ladies offering to sell mushrooms to the passers by. My English friend James had left and I decided to stay on for a few extra days before heading down to India. One day I saw a young man buying mushrooms from an old lady so when they had completed their bartering I called out to him.

"Hi," I said. "Come and tell me something," I motioned to him. "What do you do with those mushrooms, how do you eat them? I've heard that they are a type of hallucinogenic, but how do you prepare them and how does it make you feel?"

I bombarded him with so many questions, he could obviously tell I was very naïve about these things. We went and got a chai and he proceeded to tell me his experiences with mushrooms. His name was Paul. He was a dark, rugged-looking Italian guy, sexy-looking in a mysterious way. He said he only took mushrooms in a ceremonial way and didn't abuse the power of these gifts from nature. Whenever he traveled to Nepal, which was once or twice a year to buy products from Kathmandu to sell in Europe, he would come to Pokhara and buy mushrooms, prepare them as a tea, drink it and then go out into nature and commune, be one with nature and receive insights into his life.

"Wow!" I said. "Sounds very powerful. Is it dangerous?" I asked.

"Not if you do it with someone who knows," he said. "I wouldn't do it alone the first time." He looked at me for a while as if contemplating what he would say next.

"Look, if you really want to experience it, let's do it together. Come to my room and we can prepare the 'shrooms and then go take a walk."

What an amazing opportunity to experience this with someone who knows, I thought. I said yes and we left the chai shop and went back to his room. He prepared a little backpack with some water and some fruit, made us the tea and then we sat on his porch and sipped it slowly.

"OK," he said. "Let's go now before the effects really start to take hold."

We set off out of town towards the rice fields. The first thing I noticed was the color of the rice grass.

"Is it always this vibrant?" I asked, "Or is it the mushrooms taking effect?"

"I think the mushrooms are starting to take effect," he smiled and we paused and looked at the blades of rice grass dancing in the wind.

Each blade was unique and danced its own dance. It was amazing to watch. It was like one big dance party or rave! They were so fluid in their dance. I was mesmerized and felt my body wanting to move like the grass. I started to mimic the motion of the grass and then found myself amidst them, dancing with them, laughing, dancing to the music of the wind, enjoying the sun on my skin.

Continuing on our trail, we stopped to appreciate the industriousness of the ants and admired the beauty of the women clad in red cloth working in the fields, their eyes and smiles radiantly shining as they waved at us passing by. The afternoon seemed to last forever. I felt like we walked for miles but really we hadn't ventured very far at all.

We decided to head back to town pausing to rest a while on a rocky outcrop to watch the sunset. From his backpack my Italian friend brought out an orange and proceeded to peel it. Obviously the mushrooms were still heightening my senses. The smell of the orange was amazing. I could feel the zing from the skin as he pierced it with his fingers. I heard him tear the flesh apart as he prized each segment away from its sisters. I gave thanks to the fruit for giving its life force to me and savored the taste and texture as it quenched my very dry mouth.

"It's so alive," I commented as I crunched on its flesh.

"It's just as alive as a fish or an animal or any other flesh food," I marveled. I could feel its live energy surge through my cells and feed them as it passed by.

What a revelation! Fruit is flesh, meat is flesh, we are flesh. We are one and the same. We are simply flesh. The orange was so alive and I felt its life essence become me.

No more dead food for me I decided in that moment. I only want to eat that which nourishes my cells at a very deep level. No more bread, cakes, rice... only fresh, wonderful alive food. The only problem in Nepal and India though is the contaminated water that the fruits and vegetables are washed in and the unhygienic way the meat is kept and prepared.

As we wandered back into town we passed by a store which had cooked chickens and meat hanging surrounded by flies. I could hear the buzzing and see their eggs embedded in the flesh of the meat. I couldn't stomach the thought of eating anything cooked or anything that had been left out in the open to rot. What I desired was fresh fruit. Fruit wrapped up in its own skin, which protected it from the external elements.

It wasn't that Nepal was dirty, it was more that the bacteria there were different to those I grew up with, so my body was not accustomed to them. Reacting against them as if they were foreigners and not welcome, they would be expelled sometimes violently through any orifice!!

We stopped off and got some more fruit and took it back to my Italian friend's balcony and feasted on its freshness and aliveness. We both felt really hot and sticky from the walk and the heat so decided to take a shower together.

Paul was lucky to be staying at one of the few guesthouses in Pokhara that had hot, running water, which was a real luxury in that part of the world. We both felt honored to be blessed with this gift and gave thanks to the owners and the pipes as we walked towards the outside shower.

We stripped down and ventured into the shower cubicle. It's amazing how aware you become of the little things when on mushrooms, like the magic of taps, and faucets, the engineering involved in piping water from the lake, heating it in the black hoses that lined the roof of the guest house and pushing it through a showerhead that fractured the water so it sprinkled gently upon us.

The texture of the water on my skin was so good. I was thirsty, inside and outside of my body, and my skin sucked up the water. My newfound friend had a bar of natural soap and he rubbed it over my body as the water showered upon me. It was so silky to the touch, it slipped and slided in and out of every crevice, falling on the floor a couple of times.

We giggled like little kids. Aware of the water shortage we turned off the flow of water and soaped each other up, lathering the suds vigorously. We rubbed our bodies against each other in glee. I turned around and rubbed my soapy bottom against his cock and felt it respond instantly. He rubbed it between my butt cheeks and then it slipped between my legs and started rubbing my clitoris.

The sensation was incredible! So silky, so slippery, so erotic! I leaned over more and braced myself against the wall with one hand and with the other reached between my legs and tickled the head of his cock with my fingers, teasing the head at the entrance to my pussy. He slipped it in, just a little but it felt so good! He slipped it in a little more. He teased my pussy, exciting my cells but it was a bit intense trying to stand upright in the shower and not slip over. We turned the shower back on, washed the soap off, wrapped our towels around us and walked back to his room.

Paul put on a New Age CD, we laid back on the bed and relaxed, enjoying the sensation of the music entering our bodies and soothing our souls. I saw myself as a conductor, arms outstretched, conducting an unseen orchestra. My arms danced with the music and the invisible instruments responded.

All of a sudden I saw a blank canvas in front of me and my hands became brushes magically filled with neverending, always changing paint. I realized that whatever I thought of instantly manifested on the canvas. The blades of grass, the fruit, the water…

Wow! I thought, imagine if I could instantly paint the picture of how I would envisage my life to be. The brushes instantly responded painting myself, with long, flowing, blond hair, radiant smile, see-through feminine robes, dancing around the globe, touching hearts, opening minds, making love, having fun.

That really is how my life is, I thought as I surveyed my canvas. What would I like to manifest in my future? I thought. My hands, as if seamlessly connected to my consciousness, started to paint airplanes, nature and a beautiful, tall, strong man, holding my hand as we flew around the earth, making love and generating a powerful energy. An energy that would emit from us, traveling out and affecting everyone - the whole world, the universe.

Yep… that would be absolutely amazing, I smiled to myself. I reached out and felt the warm hand beside me. I tickled the fingers, then moved my hand up the inside of the arm, marveling at the newness of the sensation, the heightened state of awareness I was feeling, to touch and feel the touch in return.

I rolled onto my side and with my other hand started to very lightly stroke up the inside of my friend's leg, brushing past his balls, feeling his cock twitch slightly. He was so relaxed lying there in his blissful ecstasy.

I admired his perfect manly form. Not one little bit of fat on his body. His muscles perfectly outlined, even his ribs visible under his skin. His face looked so peaceful lying there, so serene.

I rose on my knees and continued to admire and lovingly touch his body. Stroking it and caressing its entirety.

Slowly his penis started to respond. It was as if it had a mind of its own. Its owner definitely was very content not to move one inch but to lie there in blissful harmony enjoying the sensation of being touched. However, as relaxed as he was, his penis certainly responded.

I gently caressed that beautiful muscle, admiring how silky soft the skin was and how smooth the head. I knelt down and gently kissed it and tasted the sweet secretions that were emitting from the tip. I lovingly kissed and caressed that cock until I could bear it no longer. My pussy on fire I gently lowered myself onto his throbbing love muscle and shuddered at the sensation.

All my senses were totally heightened and my awareness of every little millimeter of skin touching and penetrating mine was incredible! I spent what seemed like hours exploring my own depths with the aid of my friend's penis.

I felt as if I were inside my own vagina and could see the penis entering me, the cells expanding to let that beautiful big head enter, my pulsating G spot ripe and full, responding with every thrust... I was in orgasmic heaven. I felt as if I were on another planet, surfing the heavens, floating on high.

The music in the background was perfect, a gently rhythmic classical accompaniment to a magical performance. So different to the intense classical music I made love to with my Eastern friend in Berlin. This music was lilting, light, melodic and soothing. I felt myself drift away up into the heavens on the waves of each sound, each instrument, each note carrying me higher and higher up beyond the clouds into dream-state, floating in the ethers with my psychedelic lover.

CHAPTER ELEVEN

❤ *Sixth Chakra Activation in India* ❤

Color: Indigo
Element: Ether
Quality: Insights & All-seeing
Music: Osho Music
Activities: Awareness, Whirling, Meditating
Physical Location: Third eye, Forehead

I cannot remember the transition from consciousness to unconsciousness but awoke the next morning still wrapped in my Italian lover's arms like the roots of the Banyan tree, intertwined and inseparable. Lying there in the sun's morning glow my forehead felt as if it were pulsating incessantly. I gently raised my hand and place it over my third eye and waves of indigo/violet surged through me. All of a sudden I had a vision of me in India, wandering the cobbled streets, watching the holy men enter the temples to pray. The holiness of the land was calling me to worship.

I rolled over and wrapped Paul in my arms connecting my forehead to his. It was as if I telepathically transmitted what I was seeing to him. He opened his eyes, looked at me and said, "I think it is time for you to go to India." I thought it was pretty wild that he had tuned into what I was thinking so effortlessly. I smiled, hugging him tightly, and I thanked him for one of the most eye-opening experiences I had ever had.

Packing up my belongings I headed to the local bus station and caught the next bus to the Indian border. It was a little harsh to feel every bump and every hole in the road in my body. I felt jarred and bruised by the time I arrived at my destination, Varanassi, the holy city in India, where people from all over India and all over the world pilgrimaged to pray and give thanks. It was dirty and grimy.

The left over effects of the mushrooms from the day before were such that the sensations, smells, sights, noise and intensity of the number of people everywhere were almost too much. I wanted to escape, to find a secluded place to be, to rest my weary body and recharge. But to get to anywhere in Varanasi you had to walk and the windy, narrow, cobble-stoned streets seemed like a maze.

A young boy I met at the bus station said he would take me to a clean, comfortable place to stay, not far from the station. He guided me through what seemed like a never-ending maze of streets. The little alleyways just kept going and going. I could have sworn we were going round and round in circles. Finally I gave up and sat down on the side of the road.

"I can't go any further," I said to him. I was totally worn out, so tired. I buried my face in my hands and took a few deep breaths. When I looked up I noticed that I was sitting next to a vendor selling chai. He poured me a hot cup of tea and I sipped on it. Slowly its warmth permeated my body and I could feel the last little bit of strength I had returning, enough to be able to lift my backpack onto my shoulders and venture forth through those last few meters of narrow cobbled streets until finally we arrived at "Shangri-La Guesthouse."

It was typical Indian style. Not that clean, but clean enough for this tired traveler. I climbed the stairs to the room at the top of the building and laid down my backpack. Going out onto the rooftop I stretched my body, moving my shoulders especially as they were aching from carrying my backpack for so long. I looked out across the rooftops at the sunset and the many colored kites flying in the sky. The energy of the setting sun revitalized me enough and I found the communal shower, freshened up and went back to my room. Lying down on my bed, I drifted off into a bizarre dream state with the noises and images of the city and the strange language filling my mind.

In the early hours of the morning I awoke to a

sensation that I was not alone. I could hear rustling at the end of my bed. Trying not to move an inch, I very slowly opened my eyes and looked towards the sound wondering who had entered my sanctuary. There was just enough light coming in through the window to outline a bizarre scene. To my surprise I saw a cheeky-looking little monkey feasting on my bananas looking at me incredulously! I sat upright in amazement.

"What on earth!" I started to say, then laughed out loud. How crazy! Even a woman's bedroom is public domain for these creatures, I marveled. I sat there and watched the monkey eat its fill of my bananas then wander off onto the rooftop, hoist itself up onto the wall and jump off onto the next roof. What freedom these little creatures have, I thought. What a life!

I decided to rise, get dressed and go exploring. I was excited to be in one of the holiest cities in India and knew there would be some wonderful new experiences to be had. I had no idea where I was but decided just to head off and see where the path would lead me.

Even though it was very early in the morning vendors were out on the streets selling flowers for the temples as well as chai and sweets made of milk and sugar. Walking gingerly past a holy cow, I passed by a temple but knew I would not be welcome there.

I made my way down to the famous Ganges River and paid for a boat ride down to the burning ghats. I was shocked to my core at how dirty the river was. People were bathing in it, drinking it, washing their clothes in it. It stunk and there were all sorts of things floating down it including dead cows, trash and the most shocking sight of all, a dead baby in a wicker basket!

The smell of burning flesh as we neared the ghats was almost too much to handle. We paused so that I could see the burning bodies and the family members standing by watching and giving their prayers but then it was too much.

I motioned to the guy rowing the boat to take me to the shore. I couldn't hold on any longer. I rushed out of the boat and threw up next to a wall. Dry retching I couldn't get the smell or images of the burning flesh out of my mind.

I quickly paid the man and stumbled off down the streets until I was far enough away from the stench. Images everywhere filled my mind. People without legs begging for money, emaciated mothers with skeleton-like children, hands outstretched. I found a place that served tea and sat down continuously hounded by the people around me.

"Money Miss?" they implored. Or otherwise it was Indian men, seeing me alone, asking "Where are you from Miss, what is your name, are you married?"

I wanted to escape. I couldn't handle all these people continually wanting something from me. I hailed a rickshaw (bicycle drawn taxi) and told my driver the name of the place where I was staying and wrapped my sarong over my head, draping it across my shoulders so that no one could see my blond hair. I wanted to become invisible.

So, this is the holy city of India. Well, it's not my idea of a holy place, I thought as I reminisced about the tall snow-capped peaks of the Himalayas in Nepal, the dancing rice fields and gentle Nepalese people.

I ran up the stairs to my room and collapsed on the bed. This may be a special place for Indian people to come to, I thought, but it's definitely not my scene.

Tears of exhaustion flowed down my face. I had forgotten to shut my door and suddenly I felt another presence. Oh my God, I thought, not some other Indian person here to ask me my name and where I am from.

I buried my face into the pillow and sobbed. A man's very gentle voice spoke and it sounded like velvet. "You are overwhelmed I can tell. It is a crazy place here and can be too much for some sensitive people. Can I talk with you for a moment? I know of a place that you might like. It is a very special place where people respect your choice to be alone and quiet and there are plenty of places to meditate and enjoy the silence. I think you would like it."

He had my attention. My sobbing subsided; I raised my head, dried my eyes and looked at this sweet-natured Indian man at my doorway. I recognized him as the man at the front desk who had been so helpful when I arrived the night before. I smiled my gratitude and asked him to sit with me and tell me more.

"It is quite a way from here but worth the train trip," he said sitting tentatively on the edge of my bed.

"There is an enlightened master who has a large following of people from all over the world who come to hear his words of wisdom and sit in his energy. There is lots of dancing and fun times, but also lots of places and times to be very quiet and to go within. It is a beautiful sanctuary, very clean and peaceful. I am sure you will like it," he smiled and laid his hand on mine.

I had never felt such a gentle, soft hand in all my life. I looked up into his soft, brown eyes and melted. He had such a beautiful, peaceful nature, so serene, I folded into his arms thanking him for being there. He responded by gently wrapping his arms around me and holding me, soothing my troubled soul. We sat there for a long time, me cradled like a baby in his arms, him gently rocking me.

"Will you lie next to me on the bed and just hold me?" I asked, feeling like a little child. He slipped off his shoes and gently laid me on the bed, slipping in behind me, spooning me and holding me gently. I could feel the warmth of his body next to mine and finally felt like I could let go.

I relaxed into his arms and could feel the gentle rise and fall of his chest as he breathed lightly. I found his breath mesmerizing and blocked out all the outside sounds and focused on his breath, synchronizing my breath with his until we were breathing in unison, as one. With each inward breath I could feel my body revitalizing and filling up with renewed energy. With each out breath I could feel the tension letting go.

I visualized all the negativity being breathed out and visualized only love flowing in through my cells. Soon my body started to heat up with that familiar warmth as I felt the love flow into me from the universe and the comfort and warmth from my new friend merge into me. I rolled over and looked him in the eyes and with my mind's eye said thanks.

There was no pressure, he was just simply being present, there with me, holding me, being there for me. I felt such gratitude, I kissed him gently on the lips. The warmth of his lips against mine softened me even more as he gently returned my kiss.

I maneuvered myself so that my outstretched body could press up against his. Lying on our sides we held each other in a warm embrace and enjoyed the connection of our heart, bodies, minds and souls. We continued to breath in unison and with every inward breath I could feel my energy returning.

I wiggled my little pussy closer to his body and could feel him respond beneath his robes. I could feel the natural manly reaction to my female energy awakening. I rolled on top of him and pressed my body next to his, enjoying the sensation of something hard pushing up against my femaleness. I kissed him passionately and got more and more turned on.

He just lay there and let me grind myself against the hard cock beneath his robe. I sat up, straddled him and started to ride him, rubbing my clitoris against his manly member, working myself into a frenzy.

I closed my eyes and felt the energy building within me. Here we were totally clothed and yet it felt like he was inside me! My pussy twitched in glee as I thought, this really is safe sex! I couldn't contain myself any longer and orgasmed through my trousers onto his cock. He felt my warm juices and he instantly responded, also coming in his under-shorts. We looked down into each other's eyes and smiled.

"Thank you for helping me shift my energy," I smiled.

"Thank you for sharing your energy with me," he smiled back. "Let me tidy myself up and I will write down the information for you on how to get to Poona. I know you will love it there." He put the palms of his hands together at heart level and slightly bowed towards me, saying "Namaste," which means peace be with you, and backed out of the doorway.

What a little angel sent down from the heavens to help me, I thought and walked out onto the rooftop, opened my arms and gave thanks to the universe for looking after me.

My Indian friend whose name, I found out, was Nirav, returned and saw me standing there. He came up and gave me a wonderful hug. I turned around and hugged him back and told him I was excited by the thought of adventuring to Poona and connecting in with like-minded souls. It just felt right. I have always lived my life by that principle, if it feels right, do it. And this felt so right. I was smiling from the inside out and couldn't wait until dawn break to escape the madhouse of Varanasi and head south to Poona.

The train ride was an experience in itself. I wrapped my sarong around my head, sat next to the window and surrounded myself with a safe wall of protective energy. I didn't want to be bothered by anyone, and surprisingly it worked. I was left alone in my first class seat, in my thoughts and spent hours gazing out the window at the passing countryside, catching glimpses of Indian women clad in red saris, carrying water on their heads, or babies on their side.

We passed through many towns and it felt good to be safely encased in the train's compartment. The gentle rocking of the train on the rails lulled me into a meditative state. I closed my eyes and reflected on my travels, my experiences and focused on what I would like to experience on this next stage of my journey.

In my mind's eye I pictured a place with conscious

people, having fun, enjoying this experience of life, going inside, looking at any blockages that held them back from being all they could be, enjoying their physicality yet also relishing time alone, to go within and meditate. How I longed to be connected with others on the same frequency, to feel a sense of community, of belonging, yet to have the personal space to explore my own depths at the pace I wanted to.

Finally my train arrived in Poona and I got into an awaiting taxi and asked to be taken to the ashram. The taxi driver, with a mass of material wrapped turban-style on his head, looked at me and raised his eyebrows.

"So, you are one of those sannyasins?" he asked.

"What's a sannyasin?" I asked back.

"Well," he paused, "I suppose you would say it is a person on the path, the spiritual path to enlightenment."

I reflected a moment, then responded, "Yes, I suppose I am," and smiled to myself.

"I hear that they are very open-minded at that ashram," my driver commented.

"What do you mean by that," I asked, intrigued.

"There are lots of stories of wild sex parties, people running around naked, going crazy," he said. Well if that's the case, I thought, sounds like my kind of place!

"I have no idea," I said back to him, "but I suppose I will find out. Have you been there yourself?" I asked.

"Oh no," he replied, shocked. "I am a faithfully

married, religious man," he said with a shake of his head, "I do not condone free sex."

We drove in silence and I wondered just what it really would be like. Obviously the local people had some crazy idea of what this commune was about and it would be interesting to find out myself. That was how I lived my life. I never believed what others said, but chose to experience it myself first hand and then speak from my experience. I believe that is the way to live truthfully. I also have never liked talking about another person behind their back. I always feel it is better to talk to the person directly if I have an issue with them and to be up front and honest about my feelings.

My taxi driver dropped me off at the front gates of the ashram. I was met by a very friendly, older gentleman with a long white beard and sparkly eyes.

"Welcome!" he smiled. "Come and sit down and let me offer you some fresh, clean water. You must be dry from all this heat and your long travels."

Wow, I thought to myself. What an absolute treat this man was. I just loved his youthful energy. He seemed timeless and obviously loved his job of welcoming newcomers.

"My name is Gopal. Let me tell you about this place," he smiled and motioned to some seats close by.

"First it is necessary for you to have an AIDS test. Everyone who enters the ashram has to be certified AIDS free. It's not that everyone is having unprotected sex by any means. We definitely do not encourage that. It is simply a reminder that we need to be conscious and aware and this is part of the process. It only takes 15 minutes and while you wait I will tell you more about the place," he smiled and guided me to a very clean room where the 'nurse' gave me the test.

It felt good to know they were careful here and so I readily accepted the test. Then I sat chatting with Gopal until my results were ready. He told me about all the different meditations that were offered every day and for one entry fee I would have access to the ashram as much as I wanted from 5:30am to late at night. If I wanted to I could dance and meditate from dawn to dusk, and late into the evening hours. It sounded like a dream come true. I couldn't wait to go in and have a look around.

My results came back negative and then Gopal took me and 5 other newcomers on a personalized tour of the ashram pointing out where the main meditation hall was, where to eat, shower, locker room, where the different personal growth workshops were held. He also pointed out that anyone wearing a round, white badge on their robes was to be respected as wanting silence and not to be talked to. I really liked that idea.

Everyone wore maroon-colored robes which served to create a seamless consistency. Gopal explained that every color has an associated energy and vibration which could be distracting to others wanting to meditate. Everyone wears maroon because it is a very neutral color, the same color as the Tibetan monks wear.

I could feel the tension lifting from my head. It felt as if a great weight had been lifted from my shoulders and the curtains had been pulled back from my eyes. I breathed a sigh of relief. For some reason I felt at home here. As we wandered through the ashram, I noticed the serenity on the people's faces. I could see others standing in little groups smiling and laughing. As we passed by the communal meditation hall I saw blissful multitudes bathing in the ecstasy of their inner worlds, swaying their bodies in time to the music, eyes closed, arms outstretched.

We paused to get a drink from a "safe" water fountain and all of a sudden I felt overwhelmed with emotion. I turned to Gopal and asked him if I could have a hug. He smiled, knowingly, and wrapped his arms around me tightly, lovingly. I felt his heart connecting with mine, his body melt into my own, his breath instantly becoming one with my own. It was such a beautiful, warm, safe feeling. I wanted to stay there forever, and we did stay like that for quite sometime until I became very aware of how tired I was.

Gopal, sensing my deep tiredness suggested that I go next door, find a room and rest a little. I looked around wide-eyed, as we walked back out to the front gate. I felt like a little kid in a candy store that didn't want to leave, didn't want to miss out on anything, but I realized that I was totally exhausted and really did need to find somewhere to lay my weary head.

It was 11am and Gopal said that I was welcome to come back at 3pm and join in on the Sufi meditation he was leading. I walked next door to the big, old hotel that must have been quite something in its day. It looked a little dilapidated, but was still elegant. They did have a room, which was good as I really didn't feel like searching for anywhere else. It was a large spacious room with a big double bed and windows opening out onto a little balcony surrounded by trees.

I collapsed onto the bed, happy to be horizontal and drifted off into a meditative dream state with one hand on my heart and the other on my belly. Before I drifted off completely I gave thanks to the universe for bringing me here. Tears of gratitude flowed out the corners of my eyes and down onto the pillowcase. I felt so at peace, so happy.

For some reason it really did feel like I had arrived home. In my mind's eye I traversed the last few days as if watching the rerun of a movie. I smiled as I saw myself traveling the world searching. What am I truly looking for? I asked myself. Looking at myself traveling, I saw this beautiful woman, touching hearts, awakening bodies, surfing the etheric realms of consciousness, happy within herself but looking for something or was it someone?

Yes, I thought to myself, I am ready to meet that

special person in my life. I open myself to that possibility universe, I said inwardly. Visualizing the blank canvas of my mind, I painted the recurring image I kept getting of me flying around the planet, hand in hand with a tall, lean, good-looking man who was the other aspect of my soul. I'm ready universe, I projected from my third eye as I drifted off into a very relaxed afternoon snooze.

I awoke after a couple of hours and was feeling a bit hungry so went out of the hotel, down the road to a little coffee shop where I got something to drink and eat. Next to the coffee shop was a little store selling maroon-colored robes, so I bought one and decided to go to the meditation Gopal was leading at the ashram. I went back to my room, changed into my robe and headed off to the meditation hall.

Gopal noticed me as soon as I walked in. He was so perceptive, so aware. He made sure I stood close to him and explained the meditation in detail so that I knew what was happening. The meditation involved Sufi whirling (spinning) to some specifically composed music that was supposed to help people find their center. It made me feel a little dizzy at first but then it clicked. I soft focused on my outstretched hand and all of a sudden everything around me seemed to be a blur and I was crystal-clear and totally aware of myself in the center of the vortex of spinning.

I could have spun for hours and hours but the music started to slow down and with it the intensity of the spinning until everyone came to a standstill, then lay down on the floor and watched the energy move inside. It was the most perfect thing I could possibly have experienced at that particular stage of my journey. Sometimes it felt like I was a tornado of spinning energy, especially recently with all the changes of countries, languages, people and places. Somehow doing the external spinning (whirling) allowed everything to settle back into harmony again.

Lying on the floor I was blown away at the sensations I was experiencing and the feeling of complete harmony in my body when the little Tibetan bells were rung, symbolizing the end of the meditation. Wow! I thought, this is magical stuff and so simple! Why don't more people know about these simple meditative techniques?

I slowly opened my eyes and sat up. Gopal was there waiting for me to come to. He smiled a soft, knowing smile, helped me up off the floor and gently escorted me out of the meditation hall. We sat on a bench in the garden next to the hall, holding hands, not saying anything, just being.

After some time, I turned to him and expressed my gratitude with my eyes. His eyes were so clear and so blue. I said to him, "Gopal, I want you to take me back to your place and wrap me up in your arms and just bask in this wonderful energy."

He smiled and nodded. We stood up and holding my hand he guided me to his room which was inside one of the pyramid-shaped structures I had seen when given the tour. We climbed the stairs to the second floor and he opened the door to a very simple, Zen-like, immaculate room. I nodded and smiled. Exactly how I imagined Gopal's room to be, clear and clean energetically just like he was.

I lifted my robe up over my head and stood there naked before him. His soft eyes caressed me with their glance then he gracefully removed his robe revealing a soft, age-worn older body. We stepped towards each other. Our bodies met. We wrapped our arms around each other and stood there taking in the moment, feeling what the other person felt like, sensing their energy, smelling each other's body odor, just being conscious of who we each were.

Gopal pulled away gently and looked deeply into my eyes, then took my hand and led me to his bed. We lay on top of the bed and held each other, feeling each other's warmth and tenderness. Ever so softly we started to caress each other's skin. I marveled at how soft and silky his skin was. He honored and adored my youthful body. I couldn't work out how old Gopal was. He seemed timeless, ageless. He could have been 150 years old for all I knew.

Time had no meaning, minutes passed into hours as we tenderly caressed each other. I was so consciously aware of every little touch he made on my body, the sensations, the texture of his touch. I felt so alive, so loved, so honored. It felt so pure, so soft, so loving. When my hand caressed his penis I was surprised at how it responded. His silky head pulsated as I stroked it. Still virile, I thought to myself.

How beautiful this is, I marveled. He is one of the most beautiful people I have ever met. I felt so honored to be there with him in his sacred space. Slowly I lifted myself off the bed and let my long, blond hair caress Gopal's body from the top of his head to the tips of his toes. Then I very gently caressed his entire body with my nipples, brushing them on his feet, over his legs, between his thighs, past his beautiful hard penis, up past his nipples to his face and lips.

Lowering my body down onto his so that our toes were touching, I stretched my legs straight out on top of his, my pussy gently lying on top of his penis. Slightly propped up on my elbows our nipples connected, our lips touched and our foreheads gently pressed against each other. I could feel his chest rising with each breath and allowed my breath to become one with his.

I gently rubbed my clitoris against his hard cock and my pussy became more and more aroused. I circled it round and round in little tiny circles. Somehow my pussy maneuvered itself so that the head of his penis rested at the entrance to my vagina and as I circled my hips the softness of his head teased my pussy lips open. Slowly he worked his way into my pussy until I was gently sliding up and down his wonderful cock as our lips began to kiss, our foreheads still locked together.

The color show I was having in my third eye was

psychedelic. I could feel the energy being circled, moving up in spiral form through my pelvis, around my spine, encircling my internal organs, my belly, up past my chest, around my throat, up past my third eye to the top of my head. Then it felt as if that spiraling energy plugged itself into the top of my head, anchoring it back into my body.

We lay there spiraling the energy up and up, then back down, then up and up, over and over again until Gopal could hold it no longer and exploded his warm juice into my pussy. I could feel his cock pulsating in my pussy and instantly convulsed into a shuddering orgasm that reverberated throughout my body, sending waves of energy from my body into Gopal's and back again.

We rolled over and laid sideways on the bed, our third eyes still connected. Slowly we opened our eyes, not a word spoken between us, and pulling back slightly looked into each other's souls. Waves of emotion flooded through me as Gopal's face shape shifted and changed reflecting different emotions and faces back to me. It was like watching a movie, a fascinating movie, yet I knew that his face was simply reflecting what was happening within me.

My heart was bursting with love for this man, with gratitude for the wonderful gift he had given me, for the beautiful, welcome-home. The light was changing outside and obviously it was nearing evening.

Silently without speaking we completed our energy

exchange and smiled our gratitude to each other, gently prizing our bodies apart. We got up and showered together silently, rubbing soap over each other, caressing and honoring each other's bodies. Then we put our robes back on and left his sacred space, walking out into the mild evening air. He glanced at his watch and his eyes lit up.

"Just in time for the Sannyas ceremony in the main hall," he smiled. "What a treat for you on your first day here."

"I feel like I have been treated more than I could possibly have imagined already," I replied, "I cannot imagine more!" Gopal squeezed my hand and smiled a knowing smile, leading me towards the music.

As we walked into the hall I was overwhelmed by what I saw. A hall full of people smiling and dancing happily to the live music being played by five musicians. I couldn't believe my ears. The music was so melodic, so smooth, so serene, so harmonious.

As I tuned into the words, I shook my head in disbelief. It was as if they were singing this song just for me. It was about the journey, the search and the feeling of having found my way home. The chorus was "home is where the heart is" and I started to cry with joy. I had found my home. It wasn't here in Poona, it was a place within me, within my heart. I turned to Gopal and hugged him and we danced together as I cried my sweet tears of joy.

"You are such a sannyasin," Gopal smiled. "You are

so pure, so spiritual, so much on the path, so there! Your Indian name would have to be Pavitra," he continued, "because you are so pure."

"Wow! Thank you!" I exclaimed. "Pavitra! What a beautiful name. I love it. Can I use that name? I've always wanted a special spiritual name and that really resonates with me." I was so happy. I could have died right then and there and gone to heaven. I felt so full, so complete, so whole.

Gopal and I danced and danced and danced, smiling, laughing, hugging, ourselves and everyone else there. It was such a wonderful feeling to be surrounded by loving, conscious people.

Thank you Nirav, I said silently with my heart. My Indian friend in Varanassi knew that I would love this place. He had planted the seed and now that little seed was being fertilized, watered, loved and nourished and was blossoming into the most beautiful flower imaginable. And that flower was me. I was blossoming, opening, sharing my aroma, my essence with everyone and everything.

This is true bliss I thought as I wandered back to my hotel room after the festivities had finished and I had hugged Gopal goodnight. I lay down on top of my bed and reflected over my day - my experiences, my newfound realizations, my new name - and gave thanks. I opened my arms wide as I lay there and felt the universe pouring its love into my heart, overflowing it and melting me onto the bed.

I gave thanks to Gopal, such a special, special man who had truly activated my body, heart and soul that day. As I lay there bathed in bliss the recurring image came back to me. I saw myself floating around the planet, hand in hand with the other aspect of my soul, my twin flame. A youthful, vibrant, yet mature and spiritually aware man who had experienced life and love who was also searching for that special person to go deeper in love with.

My eyes overflowed again, this time with tears of longing. I had found me. I had found my heart, yet I knew that there was this special person out there waiting for me, to join with me so utterly and completely that we would be one.

I spent three months in Poona, loving every moment, attending all the meditations and festivities, participating in several personal growth, tantra, healing and mysticism workshops. I explored different connections with the many wonderful people I met, but each time I made love, although it was beautiful, I knew it wasn't "it."

Each person was potentially "the one" but when we connected intimately I could see that I only connected on certain levels with them. With some I would have a great sexual connection, others a fantastic spiritual or intellectual connection, but there was always something missing.

I realized that each person had different chakras that were compatible with mine, yet there was no one person with whom I had experienced ALL chakras being activated. It was fascinating making love with this awareness, or talking with someone and watching the energy and how we interacted, but at the same time it was also frustrating.

"I'm ready universe!" I would cry out into the night, to the moon, up to the night sky. "I'm ready!"

Then during one meditation I got a very strong message that I was to return home to New Zealand. My visa was about to run out anyway, so I decided it was time to return to my homeland. I had been traveling for a long time and it felt right to head back to where I had started and complete the circle.

Bidding all my wonderful friends goodbye, with a special goodbye to Gopal, I left by taxi back to the train station where I had arrived, took the train to Bombay and flew back to England where I caught up with Tim and Scott before buying my ticket back to New Zealand.

The sixth chakra is all about seeing things clearly. My time spent in India was truly insightful. I learned a lot about myself, my relationships to others, what I wanted to manifest in my life and who I was. It was time to put it all together now and get that final piece of the jigsaw puzzle in the right place. As I boarded the plane back to New Zealand I knew that I would find that final piece of the puzzle back in my homeland, that the circle would be completed and this chapter of my life's journey finished.

CHAPTER TWELVE

❤ *Seventh Chakra Activation in New Zealand* ❤

Color: Violet/White
Element: Light
Quality: Tuned In & Out-there
Music: Ethereal, New Age, Spacey
Activities: Mile High Club, Vision Questing
Physical Location: Top of the Head

As we took off to New Zealand, I visualized the big metal bird and all its passengers surrounded by light and love and arriving safely in my homeland. The plane surged down the runway. I felt myself pushed back into the seat and could feel the energy surge through my body from the base of my feet to the top of my head. Phew, I thought to myself, this is going to be a powerful trip!

After the initial take off and once the seat-belt signs had been turned off, I got up to stretch my legs and go to the toilet. I loved long flights. It always meant at least three movies and I hadn't seen any movies for a long time because I had been starring in my own – the movie of my life. My life was so intense and full and exciting that I had not even thought about movies, books or anything involving the lives of others. My life was so interesting I had no need to live vicariously through others.

I walked around the plane stretching my legs and then stood by the toilets, did some leg stretches, chatted with the flight attendants and passed the time of day with a few of the other passengers. One young lad particularly caught my interest. He was from the States and off to New Zealand to do a mountain bike tour throughout the two islands. His name was Justin. He was about 20 years old, blond, toned, had a tanned body (from what I could see) and was VERY cute. Yum yum, I thought to myself!

We started talking about traveling, all the different places I'd been to, the people I'd met, the differences in each country, each culture. Then I started to tell him my theories about making love through the different energy centers which really seemed to intrigue him. The more we talked, the more I realized that here was a very enlightened young man. Even though he was young in years he had obviously been around the universe a few times and gained a lot of spiritual maturity over many lives. He had also done a lot of mountain climbing and we compared notes about making love at high altitude. Then I asked him if he had ever joined the mile high club.

"What's the mile high club?" he asked with a sparkle in his eye.

"It's when you are more than a mile high up in the sky, usually in an airplane and it can't just be making out, oral sex or blow jobs. It has to be the full deal which can be quite challenging, especially in those small toilet cubicles," I laughed.

"Are you interested in becoming a member?" I asked innocently.

"Of course!" he responded eagerly. "But tell me how we go about doing this. Obviously we can't spend all night in the toilet and end up pissing off all the other passengers wanting to pee," he smiled.

"The best way to do it is get all worked up and excited while sitting together in the seats and then go back to the toilet in the middle of a movie when the lights are out and everyone is looking at the screen, and sneak into the bathroom and do the do," I explained.

"Sounds good to me," he replied. "Hey look, the movie's starting," he said. "Anyone sitting next to you?"

I actually had two spare seats next to me and was looking forward to lying down and getting a few hours of sleep at some stage during the long trip, so that was perfect.

The movie was quite a boring one so we sort of watched it, but mostly fooled around fondling each other. I stroked his cock through his trousers and he slipped his hand down my skirt and tickled my clitoris. At one stage I unzipped his trousers and pulled out his raging woody and bent over and sucked it a little. I could sense he was getting VERY excited and was going to pop if I didn't stop so I said to him that it was time to do it.

He eagerly jumped out of his seat and we both went to the back of the plane and squished into the tiny cubicle. I bent down on my knees, pulled his cock out of his trousers and sucked it in my mouth. Then I stood up, turned around and pulled my skirt up. Sticking his hard cock between my legs I rubbed him up against my clit and got very wet and juicy.

The plane started to wobble due to turbulence and we would have fallen over, if it hadn't been so squished. We giggled like little kids. He fell backwards and sat down on the toilet seat with a thump and I fell back onto his hard cock. It slipped effortlessly into my very wet pussy and I could hear Justin gulp.

"Whoops!" I said. "Thank goodness you were there behind me to catch my fall." I giggled. "Oh my! What did I land on?"

"My nice hard cock!" he laughed. "You got me right where you want me. I'm pinned here. Can't move!"

"Ah ha," I responded. "Now I can have my wicked way with you!" and cackled like a witch.

I proceeded to slide up and down on that nice young cock until he couldn't hold on any longer and fired his load into me.

"Oh you bad boy," I teased. "Now I'll be dripping on my seat all night long!"

"Let me lick you clean mistress," he replied already hoisting my bottom up off his cock and burying his face into my pussy. Licking wildly he slurped and sucked and licked and flicked my clitoris.

"What a good little slave boy you are," I said, taking on the role of mistress as he suggested. "Don't leave a drop, lick it all up now, you hear?"

"Yes mistress," he gulped between slurps.

"Now don't talk with your mouth full," I scolded him.

Suddenly there was a bang on the door and a voice asking how much longer we would be because there was quite a line up for the toilet. Apparently the movie had finished and we had been in there longer than we realized. Justin pulled up his trousers and I wiped my pussy dry with some paper towels. We sheepishly made our exit from the cubicle to various looks of shock, smiles, and disbelief.

We giggled our way back to our seats and feasted upon the dinner that was served by the disapproving flight attendants.

"You only live once," I said, "as far as we know for sure. So we may as well make the most of this experience called life."

"That was fun!" said Justin. "Now I know why my

parents called me Justin. I just got it in and I came!" and we laughed some more.

"I must admit I feel a little dizzy, coming at this altitude!" said Justin. "I might go back to my seat and rest a bit. See you later, and thanks again for initiating me into the mile high club. You're awesome!"

Such a cool, young guy I thought. What fun. I love life. Why don't more people live life like this and take advantage of opportunities more often. Life is too short to be serious. We need more laughter, more fun, and less seriousness.

After the dinner trays were removed I stretched out on the three seats and relaxed into a semi-meditative state. What a wonderful world this would be if more people enjoyed their physical bodies, took advantage of opportunities, did outrageous things, lived out their fantasies, and lived in uninhibited joy.

Once again the image of me and my soul mate with cupid wings flying around the planet filled my mind's eye and I said a silent "Yes" to the universe. That's what I wanted to do in my life, travel the world touching people's hearts, awakening them to the joy of life and living, showing them how they can free themselves up and experience ALL of what life has to offer.

I must have slept through the rest of the flight and awoke to the smell of breakfast being served. I got up and did some stretches down the back of the plane and met up with Justin again. He came back and joined me for breakfast and we chatted more about the meaning of life and how important it was to say YES to life and all that it offered. I knew he would have a wonderful time in New Zealand. He was going to visit some relatives first and then bike around, going with the flow, following his heart. Good on him, I thought. That's how I live my life too, and it works! I was looking forward to reconnecting with my family and friends too.

Landing in New Zealand, I had the urge to go and visit an old friend of mine, Steve. He lived on the edge of a picturesque lake in the South Island surrounded by the most amazing nature scene you could ever imagine – snow-capped mountains, clean air, crystal blue water, trees and native bush. A perfect way to 'arrive' back to New Zealand and connect in with the land. The energy there was so serene, I knew it would be a calming influence for this whirlwind traveler. Arriving at his front door I wondered if he would remember me as it had been quite some time since I had seen him.

As the door opened, there stood Steve, with a grin from ear to ear as he said, "Well, look what the cat dragged in this time! I had a feeling you would be coming to visit," he smiled.

Wonderful Steve, such a crazy "Joe normal" guy who was actually very tuned in and aware! He opened his arms wide, inviting me into his warm embrace. Wrapping me up in them he welcomed me back and offered me a cup of tea. We sat and chatted about my travels and as I started to recount some of the places I had been and experiences I had had, I realized the bigger purpose of why I felt drawn to Steve's place.

I looked up at him and said, "Can I ask you a big favor?" He smiled as if he already knew what I was going to ask.

"Of course you are welcome to stay, as long as you want to or need to," he said before I even asked the question. "Sounds like you need some time and space to absorb all your different experiences and make some sense of it all."

Tears welled up in my eyes and I thanked him. It was exactly what my heart was telling me I needed to do. Just to sit still, be quiet, look within, put all the pieces together and see what would present itself to me. I decided to do a vision quest which is a seventh chakra activation process where you reflect over your life's experiences and visualize what you would like to manifest.

I submerged myself in Steve's cozy little cottage, wrapped myself in a big, soft, cuddly duvet and leaned up against the wooden walls. I opened my journal and started to write down all the wonderful experiences I had had traveling around the world. I thought back to Australia and my aboriginal friend and the connection to the earth and my first chakra I had there. I wrote down about my experiences in Africa - being given the prized young man for the evening, the mating dance, meeting Lilou's friend and the raw, passionate, intense loving I had with him. Then I reminisced over the wonderful, sensual second chakra connections I had in France with the fruit-seller, the sea, the monsieur who took me out to dinner and then back to his mansion; and the beautiful Rastaman and waterfall in Jamaica. Then there was the powerful third chakra German man at the Berlin Wall, the fully empowered woman I made out with, and the Eastern European guy and his power plays. Next I reflected over the wonderful heart connection and fourth chakra activation I had with Paddy in Ireland and the heart opening I experienced in Egypt. Then the opening of the fifth chakra with the English twins, the crop circles and the threesome I had in England. This was followed by the throat chakra activation in Nepal with James and my third eye activation whilst on mushrooms with my Italian friend in Pokhara. Then I gained the sixth chakra awareness with Nirav in Varanassi and discovered the spiritual connection with myself and Gopal in Poona. Finally, I remembered my recent mile high experience and the recurring image I had of this mysterious soul mate that my heart and soul longed to connect with.

The seventh chakra is very much associated with visualization and manifestation, tuning into the etheric fields and tapping into the energy of things. I felt a deep longing within that I wanted to connect with my ultimate dream lover in the physical plane, and experience all that there was to experience with him.

But here I was, sitting in the little log cabin alone. I realized it was made of big, strong, hard beams of wood. I felt myself melt into the walls. The energy and strength of the wood began to permeate my bones, the softness of the beams nestling me in their embrace. I decided to enjoy this moment of aloneness and utilize my time to reflect over all the different lovers I had had.

Wood, I thought to myself, I love wood, I love strong, hard things. I love woodies! I started to smile inwardly as all the images of wood came into my mind. I like it big, hard and strong, I thought.

I prefer the big, hard solid ones to the little, soft, puny ones. I started giggling as all the images of the penises I'd experienced superimposed themselves in my mind's eye onto different types of trees: bamboo, birch, dried up old twigs, young saplings, eucalyptus, stubs, towering tall redwoods, solid strong oak.

Suddenly I felt my body waking up as the memory of each sexual experience rekindled. My mind's eye traversed the world forest remembering the different sticks and trees, their different colors and textures, smells and feelings. I relived orgasm after orgasm envisaging each woody, one after the other, feeling them re-enter me, experiencing each and its uniqueness. Not judging any of them, but just noting which felt the best. Which wood was the smoothest, strongest, softest yet hardest. Which created the most sensation. Which made me tingle and where I tingled the most.

I must have spent hours there in that little log cabin with my eyes closed, completely alone, experiencing orgasm after orgasm as I reminisced over all the lovers I had had traveling around the world. Each one had penetrated me and each one had given me wonderfully different sensations that were still a part of my cellular memory.

Wow, I thought to myself, I've had enough experiences to last me the rest of my life! All I need to do is sit here, close my eyes, take myself back to that moment and re-experience it! Does that mean I don't need anyone else anymore? I questioned myself. Well, I suppose I don't, I thought, I am completely whole and complete within myself. In essence all of that orgasmic energy is already there within me and I can tap into it whenever I want to. However, I do like the sensation of touch, I thought, but maybe just touching myself will bring back all those memories anyway. I decided to experiment…

Bringing my conscious awareness to my hands I started to touch myself gently all over. It was as if a hundred different lovers were touching me all at once. I was tingling from head to toe. I rubbed my hands over every little inch of my body, caressing my pussy, slipping one of my fingers inside my moist, wet pussy lips, gently stroking it in and out while my other hand squeezed my breasts. My vagina began palpitating with lust as memories of the different lovers I had had and the multiple orgasms I'd experienced over the years flooded back into my body. I lay there slumped against the wooden beams, bathed in glistening little globules of perspiration, my heart racing, gently moaning, waves of orgasmic bliss floating through my body, flowing effortlessly through me, igniting every cell on its path with an inner fire.

I started to feel the fire within building. It was as if every piece of wood that had ever entered me was being lit and building and building into a raging bonfire. I was on fire, literally burning from the inside out, sweat poring off my skin. I threw off the duvet and lay there drenched in orgasmic juices and perspiration, my body quivering as wave after wave surged through me.

The energy was incredible. Every cell started to melt until I was just a puddle of come juices - melting, flowing, no limits or boundaries holding the flow of the orgasmic river.

I felt my physicality melt as the fire burned. It kept burning and soon the water turned to steam. I felt myself rising like steam from a hot pool, dissipating into the air, ascending into the heavens.

Freedom! Such freedom! Floating, boundless, effortless, limitless. The immensity of the feeling was unimaginable, so big, so all-encompassing. My body lay there in that little log cabin on the edge of the lake, yet I was floating above the earth and transcending into the universe, becoming one with it.

Hours went by as I floated in orgasmic bliss and drifted on one orgasmic wave after another, lavishingly immersed in total bliss. Slowly though, as the temperature dropped outside and the cabin's internal temperature subsided, I became aware of my moist, naked body lying on the bed drenched in sweat. With a massive effort I managed to move my hand and drape the duvet over my mushy, moist body. Feeling the warmth and containment of the duvet brought me back to earth, to the awareness of my body lying there, surrounded by wood, protected by wood.

What a wonderful, safe, secure feeling. I love that sense of security I get when I am in nature, surrounded by trees. Buildings made from trees really seem to embody that feeling of strength and security too. Even though the trees have been removed from the land, they are still alive and still emit a powerful frequency of energy. Just like the sexual connections I had with all those different lovers. Even though they were no longer with me physically, their energy still lived on in my cells and the memory of our loving would be with me forever. However, I missed being wrapped up in the arms of my lover, of waking up from orgasmic loving and rolling over and looking into the serene face of a lover satisfied to their very core.

I rolled over and instead of seeing my lover beside me, I saw my journal lying there with my scribbled notes. There was a longing deep inside me for a lover I could connect with on ALL levels. I decided to make a list of all the positive things I had experienced with the many lovers I had while traveling the world. Highlighting the different chakra activations and feelings associated with each energy center waking up, I made up a wish list of what I desired in my ultimate lover.

I loved the physicalness I experienced when my first chakra became awakened in Australia and Africa; the sensuousness of the second chakra experiences I had in France and Jamaica; the power associated with the loving I had in Germany which awakened my third chakra; the warmth of the heart connections I had in Ireland and Egypt (fourth chakra activation); the expressiveness of the fifth chakra opening in England; and the awareness associated with opening my sixth chakra in Nepal and India. Now here I was in New Zealand and my seventh chakra definitely seemed to be getting activated. I was reflecting on all my chakra experiences and the seventh chakra energy was enabling me to put it all together and to learn from it all.

Lying there in my little log cabin and reading over my notes I reflected back on my most immediate experience, whereby every cell came alive with the memory of each lover I had had. It was a wonderful experience, but there was still something missing. I didn't feel completely satisfied on ALL levels. It was a mind orgasm, an upper body orgasm, not a total body, heart and soul orgasm. As I lay there I felt the recurring longing to find someone with whom I could share these experiences with totally, on ALL levels, physically, emotionally, mentally and spiritually.

I closed my eyes, put one hand on my belly and one hand on my heart and with my mind's eye put out to the universe my desire to find one person with whom I could experience all of my chakras being activated. One lover who could tap into all the different energies associated with the different chakras; who could utilize all of the qualities while making love, who would be aware of the importance of all of the energy centers being activated and not just one or two.

I wanted to meet someone with whom I connected physically, whose cock was made to fit my pussy perfectly. I wanted a lover who could touch me seductively, romance me with food and wine, and caress the tenderness of my being. I wanted a lover who could ravage me and have wild, passionate sex, who could wake me up and motivate me to do outrageous things. I also wanted a lover who would be willing to lie there with me, once I was totally satisfied, wrap me up in his arms, lovingly hold me and care for me. I wanted someone in my life who I could talk to about anything and everything, who was not afraid to express themselves. I wanted someone who was spiritually evolved and aware, who was perceptive to my needs. I wanted someone who understood their connection to all of what they are and who was willing to allow themselves to let go and merge with the universe, floating on waves of orgasmic bliss.

I wanted someone who liked to go on adventures in nature, who loved the sensory delights of nature's gifts, who was motivated about life and living, loved to cuddle and kiss, to talk about the meaning of life, was happy with who they were and aware of spiritual things. I wanted a lover who was there for me, who was strong. There to support me, hold me, wrap me up and give me a sense of security - a big tree of a man who could envelope me and penetrate me whenever I needed it. But at the same time someone who would let me run naked through the forest, yet always be there waiting for me, welcoming me back, listening to my adventures, adoring me, being there for me whatever the weather.

Looking at my journal I realized that my wish list was getting very long. When I re-read it I truly wondered if there was anyone who could possibly meet all these criteria. Perhaps I would have to make myself content with 3 or 4 lovers who could satisfy my chakra desires! Oh well, I suppose that wouldn't be too bad, I thought. It's a bit much to expect one person to have ALL those qualities. Maybe I'll just have to have a few different lovers, all at the same time!!

My eyes started to get heavy, my journal fell shut and I drifted off into a deep sleep. Awakened the next morning by a knock on my door, Steve came in with a nice, hot cup of tea.

"Guess what?" he said. "There's a big New Age gathering up the road a bit, that I think you would love. Lots of weird and wacky people, just like you, into all that energy stuff. I think you'd enjoy it... want to go?"

"Sure!" I responded. It had been quite a few years since I had been in New Zealand and this sounded like a wonderful opportunity to find out what people were up to here and also to meet some new friends. Who knows, I thought, maybe I'll find myself a few lovers to help satisfy my chakra urges!

I packed up a few things into my little backpack and we took off in Steve's truck. It was a very atmospheric day, lots of clouds, the occasional distant rain shower, with bursts of sunshine. Perfect weather for rainbows, I thought to myself.

"I'm not exactly too sure where this gathering is," said Steve. "It's apparently somewhere over the mountains here, next to a little lake. I suppose we'll just have to follow our noses and trust that we'll be lead in the right direction."

Suddenly, out of the clouds, burst the most vibrant, intense rainbow I'd ever seen. What was unusual about it was that it looked more like a thick shaft of color, rather than an arc. I couldn't see the other end of the rainbow but the end closest to us was very distinctly ending somewhere... The pot of gold? I mused.

"Let's follow that rainbow Steve," I suggested. "Maybe that will take us to where we are meant to be going."

We drove towards the rainbow, as directly as we could, crossing a few streams along the way. The rainbow started to fade, but just as we lost sight of it, we noticed some makeshift signs on the side of the road on which 'Gathering this way' was written.

"Cool!" I said out-loud. "I love how the universe works. If you are meant to find something, it will lead you towards it. You just have to follow your heart and listen to your inner guidance."

We continued to follow the signs and eventually came to the site where the gathering was. There were a whole lot of tents set up, some music playing from the main stage and heaps of people wandering around looking happy.

We paid our entrance fee, parked the truck and went off exploring. What a great scene! Lots of people, milling about, dancing and smiling. The music drew me and I made my way to the main stage. What a great group. The music they played was a mixture of African, reggae, techno and Indian, all rolled into one sound. Far out, I thought, music that resonates with all the chakras! I can tap into whichever chakra I want and dance to that particular beat, move my body and activate all my chakras with just one type of music! I like this, I thought, and started to tune into all the various rhythms and instruments, dancing myself into a frenzy.

I connected with quite a few different people who were also dancing and it was amazing to see how they moved, which parts of their bodies responded to the music, which energy center they were dancing from. I had so much fun experimenting with mirroring the different dancers and seeing how their energy felt in my body. Some were very tribal, rooted to the earth in their movements; others really focused on their hips and moved them sensuously in time to the music; others let themselves go totally and danced chaotically to the techno vibe; while others just hugged me or each other and danced slowly and intimately. This was like safe sex I thought. I can tune into where each person is at, dance with their energy, see where it sits in my body, how my body responds to them, and work out whether we would be compatible sexually or not.

Dancing is really just a vertical expression of a horizontal desire, I thought. How fascinating! Although I danced with many, many people, there was no one person that really stimulated me or with whom I felt a deep connection.

After quite a few hours of intense movement my body was dripping with sweat. The sun burst through the clouds, I grabbed my little pack and gravitated to the lake, yearning to immerse myself in the cool, fresh waters and cleanse my body and soul of the toxins I had sweated out through dancing.

I took out my beach towel and lay it down at the edge of the lake, stripped off my clothes and gingerly walked into the water, feeling the softness of it on my skin. I felt like a goddess of the underworld. Languishing in the feeling of the cool water on my still-warm body, I felt it slip through my fingers as I played with the sensation. I dived under, fully immersing myself in the lake's energy. Consciously aware of how the water allowed me to be one with it, I could feel my separateness and my connection, all at the same time. Here I was in the water, of the water, part of the water, yet different and unique.

Emerging from the mountain lake I marveled at the snow-capped peaks surrounding me. The sun glistening in my eyes, I saw the figure of a man standing on the edge of the lake obviously watching and admiring me. As I came out of the water, my nipples hard from the freshness of the lake, my naked body sleek and streamlined, I looked up and saw a tall, lean, strong man standing firmly on the earth.

"You must be cold," he said, "that lake definitely isn't tropical!" He picked up my large beach towel and wrapped it around my shoulders. As he enveloped me with his arms I felt the warmth of his body permeate me and wrap me up. I looked up into his strong, blue eyes and he paused as he secured the towel. I melted into his chest and felt no resistance as he wrapped me up in his arms and warmed my body next to his.

My heart started to pound as I felt this man's body pressing up against me. I was so aware of his manliness. My head nestled into his neck and as I turned my head slightly I brushed my cheek against the side of his face and felt the warmth and softness of his facial hair. He lowered his head and turned towards me, our lips brushing each other. I paused and felt the warmth of his breath on my lips then leaned towards him and felt the pressure of his lips against mine.

I started to kiss him and he responded and it was as if a shot of lightening shot from his lips to mine, shooting right down to the very depths of my being, igniting a fire deep within my soul. My pussy twitched in glee as I pressed my body against his and felt him wrap his arms even tighter around me. I could feel his manhood respond to my passionate kisses. I opened the towel and wrapped it around us both. He had no choice but to bring his hands inside the towel and pull me tightly towards him as I pulled the towel around his neck with my hands. His warm hands caressed my naked beauty. He reached down and grabbed my butt cheeks, squeezing them with his big, strong hands, pulling my pussy hard against his growing member. I felt his powerful energy and shuddered.

"You are the most divine goddess of nature I have ever encountered," he murmured into my ear. He started to caress my skin beneath the towel.

"You are perfect in every way… your soft skin, your perky little upright breasts." One hand held me tightly while the other explored my body, caressing my upright nipples as he continued to serenade me with his voice, "Your belly," he said as his hand gently caressed my belly button sending shivers up my spine, "…your natural bush," his hand moved down and brushed my pubic hair.

"So soft…" he murmured. Then his other hand reached up and started to gently caress my face as he looked into my eyes.

"Your eyes… so clear, your lips, so full…" He touched his lips against mine sending yet another shock of energy right down to my pussy. He must have felt my pussy twitch beneath his other hand. He slipped his fingers between my legs and felt the moistness.

My towel dropped to the ground. It was pretty obvious that I couldn't help but respond to his words and caresses. I reached out and felt the woody in his trousers growing. With my other hand I undid the button at the top of his trousers. Unzipping them I reached in. He wasn't wearing any underwear and his trousers fell to the ground. His cock leapt out of its confinement obviously happy to be free. I stroked it, marveling at how silky and smooth it felt. Gently I dropped to my knees to admire his manhood.

Wow! What a specimen! Perfectly straight, wide, long,

smooth and hard. Talk about hard! I had never felt such a hard cock. This man must be made of steel, I thought. Then I looked up into his soft, blue eyes and knew that even though his cock was like steel, his heart was as deep and welcoming as the pristine lake I had just emerged from. While gazing into his deep, blue eyes my tongue gently kissed the head of his cock.

What incredibly smooth skin he has, and sweet, I marveled. There was a sweet secretion from the head of his penis which tasted like nothing I had ever had before. It was nectar to my mouth. I devoured it, all the time keeping my eyes connected to his.

So big, so wide, I noted. As he penetrated my warm, juicy mouth with his cock, my pussy responded as if it were she that were being penetrated with every thrust. With each mouthful of this man of steel that I took, my body felt as if it were devouring him.

He pulled off his T-shirt, reached down and pulled me to my feet. We stood face to face and I realized I was at the perfect height for his hard cock to nestle itself between my legs, gently rubbing against the moistness of my pussy lips. His hands ran down my spine and grabbed my buttocks again hoisting me up and onto his shaft. He was so strong, and I felt so light and effortless in his arms. My pussy was so wet and juicy his cock just slipped right in as he lowered me down onto his raging hard-on.

Now this man really fits me, I thought. It's the most

perfect fit I have ever experienced. I couldn't believe it. I felt like Cinderella trying on the shoe that fitted. Effortless.

His perfect rod of steel filled me up and stretched me gently to my maximum capacity. My pussy responded to the new, yet absolutely perfect energy by orgasming on the spot as he entered me. I gushed and he felt my warm juices slide down his shaft. I wrapped my arms around him and my fingers slipped through his hair.

Our lips locked, his strong arms pulled my chest tightly towards him and I could feel his heart beating strongly. He carried me over to the soft, grassy patch next to the lake and gently lowered me, staying connected the whole time. His knees now resting on the ground, he was able to fully thrust his shaft into my open and receptive pussy. And I took him! Every inch of him! Welcomed him! Devoured him!

Looking into each other's eyes I could feel another energy surge pump through my body. He felt it too and responded by shafting me deeper and deeper. Our breath became stronger and stronger and soon we were breathing as one, harmoniously undulating our bodies together, the energy flowing from his penis, into my vagina, spiraling like a kundalini snake up my spine, through my lips into him.

It felt as if an electric circuit had been plugged in and we were locked in an infinity symbol of pure fire energy flowing through our cells, awakening every part of us. Consciously aware of every little sensation pulsating through our bodies, we became one, physically and energetically.

I remembered the night before in my little log cabin when my body was on fire and I had melted into the universe. The same was happening now yet I was not experiencing this alone, but with this gorgeous man. He entered my body, heart and soul, igniting me so much that every cell felt on fire. It was as if he had the key and had slipped it into my lock and unlocked the door to it all. Everything! Every possible sensation, every imaginable feeling. This man had the key!

Wow, I thought, I've found the key that fits my lock! The intensity of the fire within grew and grew until the build-up was almost too much to handle. At that point of no return he exploded his energy into me and I could feel it flowing through every cell in my body. Each cell it touched responded with a big orgasmic "Yes! Yes! Yes! Yes!" They all cried in unison. "Yes! This is it!"

"Oh my God," I cried. "This is incredible!"

Lying there on the earth still wrapped tightly in each others arms it felt like we were ascending and expanding out from the lake in the middle of the South Island of New Zealand and lifting above the earth soaring like birds floating effortlessly high on the warm winds of time, higher and higher and higher. Our physicalities strongly rooted together, our souls soared to heights neither of us had ever experienced in our lives.

The recurring image I had been having manifested itself and here I was, with my soul mate, circling the earth, spreading our love energy out into the universe. Wow! This was it!

Slowly we brought our awareness back down to our intertwined bodies, realizing that neither of us knew where one began and the other left off. Slowly opening our eyes we looked at each other in amazement.

"My angel sent down from heaven," he said, his words feeling like velvet on my skin.

"My fearless knight and his faithful steed," I responded, as it truly seemed like he had ridden in on his horse, whisked me up in his arms and carried me off to the warmth of his heart.

"Looking at you, is like looking into my own soul," he said.

"Lying here with you, I can't work out where I end and you begin," I smiled. "We are one! I don't want this feeling to ever end," I said, tears of joy welling up in my eyes.

"It doesn't have to," he responded. "I, too, have been searching for you. I knew this feeling was possible, I've dreamed of this moment. I have been waiting for this and now that I've got it, I'm not about to let it go."

We squeezed each other tightly, lying there in each other's arms, relishing the feeling of connectedness, knowing that this was the real thing. It was undeniable, unquestionable, undebatable. This was it. This was what I had been searching for my whole life. I had found me, and now I had found the other aspect of my soul. It felt as if the yin and the yang had finally joined and would never be separated again. The wholeness of our union, the harmony of our connection was beyond what I ever could have imagined.

I closed my eyes and it felt as if the whole universe was giving us a standing ovation, clapping, wolf-whistling their appreciation at us succeeding in our searches, of finding each other. It was as if the heavens were smiling on us, the Gods were happy, the birdsong sounded louder and the sun streamed down upon us bathing us in its warmth.

We lay there in bliss and talked for hours and hours, until the sun started to set. He told me that his spiritual name was Heart Eagle and that he had also been traveling the world searching for his soul mate. He had been in America when he got a really strong message that he was to return home, that someone was waiting for him. I told him all about me, my life, my travels and my message to return home too. It was like meeting up with an old friend. We felt so comfortable in each other's energy.

We could have stayed like that forever but the warmth of the day was dissipating so we decided it was time to get dressed and head back to the party. What an awesome day! I was soooo happy! We held hands and walked around the campsite. I was so blissed out just being with him.

We ran into Steve and he took one look at us and said, "So, looks like you found what you were looking for!"

"And more!" I smiled back at him.

Steve gave us both a hug and invited us over to his truck for some food. He had set up his barbeque and the coals were glowing, just waiting for the food to be put on to grill. Realizing how hungry we both were, we feasted on Steve's homegrown, killed-with-honor steak, his garden fresh tomatoes and organic salad, and sipped on his homemade red wine.

"Life is good!" we toasted as we raised our glasses and gave thanks for the gifts from nature, the magical day, old friends and new.

"She's a firecracker, that one," Steve said, referring to me. "Hope you can handle all that passion!"

"I am sure I will!" smiled my new friend. "And I'm not about to put this wild filly in a chorale. She can gallop around to her heart's content, but I will always be the stallion she runs home to."

Steve raised his eyebrows and looked at me with a sparkle in his eyes. "I think you've found the one for you, haven't you?"

All I could do was nod my head in agreement and smile the biggest smile that radiated from the depths of my soul. Yes, I had found THE most incredible man. One who lit my fire, touched my heart and connected with my soul. He felt like my rock of Gibraltar but at the same time

I could sense that he also offered me a freedom to be me that I desperately needed too. I knew at a core level that this man wouldn't want to control me, own me or possess me jealously. I could tell he would prefer to see me running naked through the forest, looking after me with eyes of admiration, honoring me for who I was, allowing me to blossom into the total woman I am but until this moment had not allowed to fully manifest.

Heart Eagle and I connected our base chakra with raw passionate love making. The softness of his touch and his sensuousness satisfied my second chakra desires. We were able to exchange power plays while we made love, flipping from me in control, to him in control, activating the third chakra. We could lie in each other's arms for hours on end, just happy to be loved and held, lying in the energy of the heart (fourth chakra). We could talk and talk and talk utilizing the throat chakra (the fifth chakra) to its absolute potential. We visualized our future, painting the canvas of our third eye (sixth chakra) with images of love and ecstasy. We transcended our physical bodies and floated on the clouds of bliss, merging with one another seamlessly, activating our seventh chakra.

We connected on ALL levels. Every chakra felt activated, satiated, whole and harmonious. Yes, this beautiful man filled my cup up completely. I have found the shoe that fits, I realized, the hand that fits the glove, the key to fit my lock, unlocking the door to a universe of love

and energy that few experience but everybody has a right
to manifest.

After feasting we went back and danced. When I
danced with my beloved it was like dancing with myself.
We could play with the energy and the music, flipping
from tribal to etheric, sensual to high energy. When we had
danced until we could dance no more we went back down
to the lake and enjoyed the serenity of it. The water energy
calmed my internal fire. We sat, snuggling up next to each
other, just being. It was amazing how calm I felt, how at
peace my soul was. I was happy just to sit there in the arms
of my beloved and feel my heart beating in time with his.
We were one. One breath, one heart, one love.

The sky started to change color and we sat and
witnessed the most magical sunrise ever. I turned to Heart
Eagle and looked deeply into his eyes. We touched our lips
and foreheads together and breathed in the fresh morning
air.

"Thank you," I vibrated through my lips into his.

"Thank you, my Goddess!" He replied.

We kissed and melted into each other's bodies
again, passionately embracing. The energy started to rise.
Without speaking a word we both stood up, started ripping
each other's clothes off, madly kissing each other all over,
slurping, sucking, licking, biting. It was as if we wanted to
eat each other up. I ravaged his cock and he devoured my
pussy. He entered my dripping, wet pussy with his raging

hard-on and I gasped. It truly was the most perfect cock and it really did fit me soooo perfectly!

We rolled around on the earth, playing like tiger cubs joined at the hips. We rolled into the water and shuddered at its coolness. Like dolphins we continued to play in the water, connected, frolicking playfully like dolphins do. The sun was starting to rise and it glistened on the water's surface. He slipped out of me and I swam to shore, pretending to escape from him. He swam vigorously after me and chased me up the beach to the grassy knoll.

Tackling me from behind I stumbled onto the ground. He dived on top of me and entered me from behind, shafting me hard and fast. I wiggled my bottom against his hard cock and felt my love juices flowing down his shaft. I managed to turn sideways and raise my knee so he was doing me from the side and could reach down and suckle on my nipple. I continued to maneuver myself around, cock firmly rooted in my pussy, and lay on my back, looking into his eyes.

The intensity of his thrusting slowed a little, he leaned down and kissed me tenderly on my lips, gently sliding his cock in and out of my pussy. I surrendered to his love, opening my arms wide, feeling the universal love energy flow through my heart into his and back to me.

What a beautiful dance of love energy, I thought. This man makes love so totally, so completely, so perfectly.

My lower chakras activated, the energy flowed into my

heart and on up into my third eye. I opened my eyes and looked penetratingly into his clear, blue eyes. The intensity was amazing. With each shaft of his penis into my pussy I felt his energy surging through my body. I started to voice my pleasure, moaning orgasmicly. He responded by grunting louder and louder with each penetration.

We built and built the energy, holding each other's gaze, feeling the crescendo heightening. Then simultaneously, at the height of the plateau we exploded into the most intense orgasm I had ever had. I screamed in ecstasy. He screamed in pleasure as his fluid shot into my welcoming cervix.

Collapsing on top of me, we lay there, feeling each other's heartbeats, breathing each other's breath. Slowly we separated and holding hands, lay on the grass and felt the sun's glow. My heart felt as big and radiant as the sun itself. The energy between us transcended the physical, connecting our auras. Each and every chakra was so totally activated, the feeling was AWESOME!

This is definitely the ultimate sex of all, I thought. This is "Soul Sex!"

"Climb every mountain, forge every stream. Follow every rainbow, till you find your dream."

SUGGESTED INTERACTIVE ADVENTURES

Yes, this story is a very erotic fantasy interwoven with elements associated with our energy centers (chakras). Many of us are searching for something special in our lives and can resonate with our intrepid traveler who traveled to exotic lands in search of the ultimate sex of all – Soul Sex. She found it and is an inspiration to all.

Here are some suggestions of how you can awaken and activate your energy centers and prepare your body, heart and soul for Soul Sex.

Be truly uninhibited and free
Do outrageous things
Live life to the fullest
Manifest all that you desire

❤ *Interactive Adventures for the First Chakra:*

Earth Ecstasy

Re-establish your connection with Mother Earth and the sensuality of the soil. Go for a trip into the desert, far away from civilization. Strip off naked, feeling the earth under you toes and slowly make love to the earth, feeling her deep connection to the power within you.

Do the Dijaredoo

If you or your partner ever get the chance to learn how to play the dijaredoo, take it! Then experiment with playing the dijaredoo over each others bodies, feeling the vibration enter deep within, activating your first chakra.

Muddy Massage

Keep your ears open for any mud baths near where you live or make a special trip to somewhere you can have private access to a mud pool. Experiment with self-massage using the mud, mutual massage with your partner and masturbating in front of each other.

Wild Walkabout

Organize an 'unplanned' vacation where you go with very few possessions, maybe just a small backpack, and see where the wind blows you. Go with the flow, don't make any plans or commitments, just allow yourself two or three days to completely remove yourself from your normal lifestyle and see where your feet take you!

Remember to pack some condoms – in the real world it is important to be prepared and protect yourself.

The Mating Dance

Imagine yourself as part of a sexual union ritual where you dance your sexuality, expressing your total femininity or masculinity, as part of the mating game. If you would like to do this with your partner - fantastic! Try seducing your partner with dance and vice versa. See how you really fit energetically. Play with it and have fun.

Dancing the Divine

This can be done anywhere, anytime. Simply find some really good drumming music and let yourself go into the rhythm until the dancer is lost and only the dance remains.

❤ *Interactive Adventures for the Second Chakra*

Fruity Fantasies

First alone, then with your lover, create a feast of fruit. Take the time to smell each fruit, feel its texture and tune into which one is the most appealing. Then, with total conscious awareness, open the fruit, breath in its aroma, touch it sensitively with your tongue and explore its depths, experiencing it completely as it becomes you.

To fully experience the texture of different fruit, try rubbing it over each other's naked body, noting the different sensations. Take turns playing with inserting different fruits into your vagina (and other places) and feel their uniqueness.

Seaside Sensitivity

Plan a holiday to the seaside and explore the sensuality of salt water and surrender yourself to its anti-gravitational force. Play with your loved one in the water and feel how limitless and unrestrained you can be. Whisper seductive French nothings into one another's ears and enjoy the stimulation and sensation of getting sexual in public!

Moonlight Magic

Next full moon invite your beloved out for a candlelit dinner for two at a classy restaurant that plays romantic, soft background music. Enjoy the sensation of every morsel of food as you sensuously devour each mouthful. Play with feeding each other and sharing wine through the mouth. Take a moonlit walk outside, being aware of how the light changes the mood, reflects on water, or enhances the romanticism. And remember you girls – appropriate outfit for a romantic evening would be a short sexy, tight dress, no bra and no panties!

Jacuzzi Joy

Make a date with your lover and go to a jacuzzi for the evening and enjoy the warmth of the water, feeling it relax every part of your body. Afterwards allow some time to lie back and feel the letting go of every cell as you relax into the moment. Take turns to gently massage some oils back into the skin, making sure to sensuously touch every part of the body, lovingly enjoying the newness of the sensation. Explore your lover's body as if for the first time.

Watery Wonders

Search out waterfalls and watery places in summertime, where you can go and enjoy the serenity of nature, the sounds of the water singing, and the sensuality of the water's caress. Take off all your clothes, give yourself permission to feel the water kiss you, and allow yourself to touch yourself, exploring different, new ways of awakening your sexual energy. Remember to give thanks to yourself, your body and nature for the wonderful gift of life.

Reggae Roll

Play some reggae music and let yourself dance freely, feeling the body relax, letting go into the rhythm, surrendering to the music until the body feels deeply at peace and relaxed.

Sexual Sunrise

Merge with the orange hues of the morning sunrise and imagine that color permeating your sexual center.

Mango Massage

Mangoes are great for this but you can also experiment with different fruits. Orange is the color associated with the second chakra so try out the different fruits of that color. Play with massaging the fruit onto different areas of your lover's body and then lick it off. Tease your loved one with the fruit, sliding it in and out of both sets of lips as you gently caress them with sensuous touch.

Beforehand, or at another time, experiment with feathers and take turns in receiving, allowing yourself to totally lie back and enjoy without any expectations of having to respond or perform.

Remember, organic fruit is the best! And when you are out having these wonderful experiences with someone other than your partner, do not forget the condoms (never leave home without them)!

❤ *Interactive Adventures for the Third Chakra*

Techno Trance

Find some full-on powerful techno dance music and let yourself go, get really into it, get hot and sweaty and feel the fire build up within you. Try putting this type of music on in the background when you make love and tap into the intensity of that type of music.

Woman to Woman

This is what is called 'safe sex' if you are a woman and is quite often less threatening to your male partner if you tell him that you are wanting to explore sexually with another woman. Either ask a good friend if she is willing to explore with you, otherwise when you are next out at a party or coffee shop and you see a woman who is attractive, go up and start flirting with her. Another suggestion is to go out to a bar that has a dance pole and get up and dance dirty with one of the other girls. Have fun with it. Be outrageous. Let yourself go.

Terrific Threesomes

If your partner is open to it, ask them if they would like to explore inviting another person into your love nest. Either another woman or a man, whatever your partner feels comfortable with. Great fun!

Animal Antics

When making love tap into what animal you resonate with and act out the characteristics of that animal. Invite your partner to also choose an animal and play at interacting physically like animals.

Power Play

Take turns being the active lover or the passive lover. Swap roles and see what it feels like to take control or to be controlled. Get into it fully and then afterwards share with your loved one which role you felt more comfortable in. It is good to be able to flip and access both sides of your third chakra, to be the one in control or to allow yourself to surrender to your lover.

Rough Wrestling

To fully activate your power center, pretend you and your partner are pro-wrestlers, get rough with each other, roll around on the floor, rip each other's clothes off, really tap into your power and let it manifest through every cell in your body. Feel your strength and let it be expressed.

❤ *Interactive Adventures for the Fourth Chakra*

Horsing Around

Find out a place where you can hire a horse and go horse riding with your beloved. Ride on the same horse together and squeeze your lover tightly from behind, pressing your body up close. Feel the vibration of the saddle between your legs and allow the exhilaration of going fast to get you excited. Whisper sexy words into your lover's ears, holding onto them tightly, telling them that you want to make love to them out in nature. When you are both totally aroused, get off the horse and make love, feel your hearts beating as one, lovingly touch and honor each other. The fourth chakra is about getting close.

Wind Dancing

The element associated with the fourth chakra is air. On a deserted beach or out in the middle of nature, take off your clothes and feel the air on your skin. Tune into the air, allow your arms to wave in the air like the branches of a tree. Let yourself become one with the air and respond to it. Let it move you as if you are a tree getting blown by the breeze.

Honoring each other

The heart chakra is all about honoring ourselves and our loved ones. It is a gentle energy, very heart-centered, loving and caring. Take turns to lovingly touch and honor your lover's body, exploring every crevice, every curve, every part of the body. As you do this, speak words of appreciation to your loved one. Tell them how beautiful they are, how much you love the texture of their skin, their shape. Focus on all the things you adore about them.

Kinky Kissing

After you have lovingly honored your partner's body, then kiss them all over, not missing one little inch of their body. Then lick them and make noises as if they are chocolate or ice cream and that you find them sooo yummy. As you are receiving the kisses and licks, let yourself respond by oohing and aahing your appreciation, loving them totally!

Hugging and Healing

After your lovemaking spend some quality time just hugging your beloved, connecting your hearts. Just lie there holding each other and feeling that love connection.

❤ *Interactive Adventures for the Fifth Chakra*

Wining and Dining

Take time each day to sit down with your beloved and talk to them about how you are feeling, what your day has been like. Make sure to ask them how they are feeling, what they have been up to, and listen to them as they speak, acknowledging what they have to say. Communication is a very important part of any relationship and sometimes this has to be fostered. Taking time to sit together and eat a meal and chat about the day, or the meaning of life while sipping on a glass of wine, can be very healing. This is definitely one way of activating the fifth chakra.

Naughty Noises

When making love really make an effort to express what you are feeling with noises, oohs and aahs. Try talking dirty to your loved one, telling them how you love their body, their cock, their pussy. Experiment with telling them what it is you want them to do to you. Whisper in their ears all the naughty things you want to do. Really activate your throat chakra while making love. When you orgasm, scream and encourage your lover to also scream. Have fun making love and making noises while you have sex.

Selfless Self-pleasuring

In order to feel more comfortable making noises when you are with your loved one, practice on yourself first. Try touching yourself all over. Work out what you like the most, soft and tender, or rough and hard. Practice opening your throat chakra and talk to yourself, make noises, express your appreciation to yourself, to your body. Lovingly touch your body all over.

Voicing Vibrations

Get your lover to sit in a chair or upright on the floor and straddle them with one leg on either side so that your base chakras are connected but you are face to face with the other person and your lips are touching. Start humming and feel the vibration travel from your lips to theirs. Feel the vibration reverberate throughout your whole body. Follow the vibration with your awareness. Feel it activate your base chakra, then move up to your second chakra, your third, your heart center and up to your throats. After doing this for some time, gently separate and lie next to each other and continue to feel the vibration in your body, even after you have finished humming. Sound is the element associated with the fifth chakra so whatever you can do to activate your throat chakra is great for activating the fifth energy center in your body.

❤ *Interactive Adventures for the Sixth Chakra*

Clothed Cuddling

Fully clothed, make out and get all hot and juicy. Rub each other through your clothes. See how far your can get with your clothes still on. If possible work each other into orgasmic frenzy while still dressed. Focus on building the energy from within. Clothes don't matter. You can make each other come just by stimulating your inner energy. This can be very erotic.

One Breath

Lying naked on the bed, wrapped up in each other's arms, connect your chakras together and especially connect your heart and your third eye. Become aware of each other's breath and synchronize it so that you are breathing together. Lie like this for as long as you can, becoming one through the breath.

Mirrored Reflection

Sit comfortably and look into each other's eyes. Soft focus your eyes so that you are looking in between your lovers eyes, at their third eye. Try not to blink and sit there looking at each other for as long as you can. Just sit and watch, seeing what images come to you. Your lover's face is like a mirror and what you see is a reflection of you. Witness your emotions, your feelings and just watch the different faces and expressions in your lover's face. When you cannot do it any longer, thank your lover, hug them and spend some time talking about what you saw.

Creative Canvas

Play some classical music in the background and visualize a blank canvas in front of you. Close your eyes and use your hands as if they were brushes. Paint the canvas with images of what you would like to manifest in your life. Paint yourself, paint your loved one, paint where you would like to be. Visualize whatever you would like to manifest in your life. Visualizing is a powerful force associated with activating the third eye.

❤ *Interactive Adventures for the Seventh Chakra*

Mile High Madness

Either plan a trip somewhere with your beloved or take advantage of the next time you are traveling together and join the mile high club. Talk about it and get each other motivated and excited. As you take off into the air, hold each other's hands, then start to get each other excited by kissing, fondling and whispering naughty things into each other's ears. When the seat belt sign goes off, get up and go to the back of the plane. Go into the toilet together and maneuver yourselves so that you can get penetration. Either get him to sit on the toilet seat and you sit on top, or he could shaft you from behind. Make sure it's a quickie so that not too many people get annoyed waiting in line outside to use the bathroom!

Manifesting your Dreams

One of the elements associated with the upper chakras is to be able to dream about what you would like to happen in your life such as the type of house you'd like to live in, the ultimate partner you'd like to be with, the holidays you'd like to take, the job you've always wished for, the money you've always desired to do the things you've always wanted to do.

Look at your life and the areas you are not happy with and set about creating a list of goals, of desires, of fantasies you would like to achieve. Spend some time writing down your dreams about the life you would like to live, the person you'd like to love and the person you'd like to be.

Sexual fantasies

What type of sexual fantasies do you have in your life? Be outrageous, think of the craziest sexual scene you could ever imagine and write it down.

Next step is to enact your fantasies, one at a time. Slowly start with something small like going into a lingerie shop and buying yourself something really sexy to wear, then visiting a sex shop and buying a little toy that you have always dreamed of trying out. Going up to an attractive stranger and asking them if you can join them at their table and then let it get wilder and wilder.

Try new things at home, with your loved one. Talk about your fantasies with your beloved. Pick up someone in a bar. Take a stranger home and have sex with them. Make out in the back of a car or in a public place. Invite someone home to join you and your partner. Go to a swing party.

Be outrageous! Try new things. Don't judge yourself. Put it all down to experience. You never know until you try. If you like it put a tick next to it. If you didn't feel comfortable put a cross next to it. If it stimulated you and excited you put three ticks next to it.

Being Uninhibited

Being uninhibited, letting the energy flow is the healthiest thing you could ever do for yourself. Look at your life and see where there are restrictions. Any denial or suppression will result as a downstream health problem so look at any aspect of yourself or your life that you have denied and set about reversing that pattern. Do the opposite for while. Explain to your loved one that this is what you need to do, that it doesn't detract from them but in order to be a whole person you have to experience this particular thing.

A scenario may come up where you think, "OK I'll try this out," and then afterwards realize that wasn't a flavor you really liked after all. But at least you tried and now you know. If you never try, then you'll never know for sure and you'll always wonder, "What if I did really like that flavor?" The denial of the experience of that flavor will always gnaw away at you from the inside and you will never feel fully complete. The seventh chakra is about completeness, so do whatever you can to activate all your energy centers and free yourself up to be all that you are.

❤ *Dancing the Chakras*

One way to activate the chakras is through movement and music. Create a compilation of your favorite music, that you can dance and make love to. Choose music that you feel resonates with the different energy centers:

1st chakra – African drumming

2nd chakra – Reggae

3rd chakra – Techno Dance

4th chakra – Celtic or Love Songs

5th chakra – Tibetan Chant

6th chakra – Indian Classical

7th chakra – New Age

❤ *Summary of Chakra Activation Process*

When you are reading Soul Sex, tune into which of your own chakras need activating and dance to that particular type of music, wear that color, eat foods of that color and practice the suggestions outlined above to activate that energy center. Play around with these ideas or make up your own chakra activation ideas. Try whatever works to activate your energy centers completely and totally so that you can be all that you are and attract that special person (or persons), into your life, so that you too can experience the ultimate sex of all - Soul Sex!